He

Mecca's Mission

Hell's Diva:

Mecca's Mission

Anna J.

www.urbanbooks.net

Urban Books, LLC
97 N18th Street
Wyandanch, NY 11798

ISBN 13: 978-1-61062-598-4
ISBN 10: 1-60162-598-7

First Mass Market Printing May 2014
First Trade Paperback Printing October 2010
Printed in the United States of America

10 9 8 7 6 5 4 3 2 1

This is a work of fiction. Any references or similarities to actual events, real people, living, or dead, or to real locales are intended to give the novel a sense of reality. Any similarity in other names, characters, places, and incidents is entirely coincidental.

Distributed by Kensington Publishing Corp.
Submit Wholesale Orders to:
Kensington Publishing Corp.
C/O Penguin Group (USA) Inc.
Attention: Order Processing
405 Murray Hill Parkway
East Rutherford, NJ 07073-2316
Phone: 1-800-526-0275
Fax: 1-800-227-9604

For Nyser and Tynayjah

Anything is possible when you put your mind to it. Believe in your dreams!

Also By Anna J.

Novels

Snow White: A Survival Story
My Little Secret
Get Money Chicks
The Aftermath
My Woman His Wife

Anthologies

Divas, Diamonds, and Dollars
The Bedroom Chronicles
The Cat House
Flexin' & Sexin': Sexy Street Tales Vol. I
Fantasy
Morning Noon and Night:
Can't Get Enough
Fetish
Stories to Excite You: Ménage Quad

Prologue

"You got in way over your head, Mecca," Tah shouted as he paced back and forth in front of the bed. He had the look of pure evil on his face, and a harsh scowl that made his handsome face look ghoulish, hardly resembling the guy who women fell head over heels for.

"Tah, what are you talking about?" Mecca cried. She couldn't believe the state she was in either. Never ever get caught off guard, that was the motto, but tonight she got caught slipping in a major way.

"You're not your aunt, Mecca. She's gone!"

"Put the gun away, Tah, and untie me, nigga. You high on them pills?" Mecca lay naked on the king-sized bed in her Hamptons villa apartment, struggling to get loose from the ropes that were tied to her wrists and ankles. Tah, her boyfriend of five years, stood at the foot of the bed pointing a chrome .50-caliber, Desert Eagle at her.

"Bitch, I ain't your flunky! You hear me?"

"Tah, who the fuck said you was a flunky? You my peoples, nigga, not no flunky! You listening to them lame-ass niggas you be with, and they put this shit in your head. Be your own man, motherfucker!"

"Fuck you, Mecca!"

Boom! Boom! Boom! Mecca felt the first slug slam into her forehead, then everything went black, and a few seconds later she saw a bright light. In the bright light she noticed a silhouette walking toward her. When the person got closer, Mecca stared into the eyes of a tall, bronze-colored man with a perfectly round Afro, and a long, neatly shaped beard. The whites of his eyes looked as if there were flames burning behind his pitch-black pupils. His long, white robe looked as if he never moved in it. There were no signs that he traveled in it. When he spoke, his voice sounded as if he were in Mecca's ears. It was like she had headphones on, and the volume was turned up to its maximum.

"I've been expecting you, Mecca. I'm glad you could make it," the man chuckled.

Mecca looked down at his feet. The color of his feet matched his face, and his toes looked as if he had the best pedicure Mecca had ever seen. His nails were evenly trimmed and glowing. Mecca didn't have a foot fetish, but if ever she'd seen feet like that on a nigga she dealt with, she would have sucked his toes without hesitation. Bringing her eyes back to his face, she gave the strange man a puzzled look. One he seemed to find amusing.

"Am I dead?" Mecca asked nervously.

"Are you dead? Are you dead? Physically, a few minutes ago, you died." The man paused, shaking his head. "Mentally, you have been dead almost all your life."

"What is that supposed to mean, and who are you anyway? What, you Jesus or God or somebody? Get it over with and take me where I'm going," Mecca responded, her fear quickly turning to anger at what the man had said.

She knew Tah had killed her and wished she could be brought back to life if for only a second so she could send him straight to hell. She hated Tah, and the feeling grew stronger as the years had gone by. She knew eventually one of them would have to die; she was just pissed he got to her first.

"So many questions," the man said sarcastically. "I love your feistiness, Mecca. We'll make the best of friends, just please don't mistake me for that Jesus guy. And no, I'm not God. You're not on his good side, Mecca."

"So you're the devil, and I'm going to hell?" Mecca asked after sucking her teeth.

"We don't use the word 'devil' around here. That's a word man made up to separate himself from the evil that exists inside of all men. We don't play word semantics, either. It is what it is. I'm just someone who knew that the evil inside of men would prevail over the good inside of them," the man laughed. "You see the semantics man used to hide what's inside of them? They put a 'd' in front of 'evil' and added an 'o' to 'God'; hence the words 'good' and 'devil'."

"What's all that got to do with me?" Mecca asked.

"Mecca, you let evil prevail, proving me right. And you know what? You had so many opportunities to go the other way, but you didn't see the signs."

"What signs? I ain't see any signs!"

"Of course you didn't. So many people around you let evil prevail, but even the people who let the evil prevail were signs for you to go the other way. You didn't take notice."

"I don't know what you're talking about," Mecca said, frustrated.

"I know you don't. That's why I'm here. I'm going to show you the signs, and when I'm done, hopefully you'll be able to accept your future. Judgment day is near," the man said while rubbing his hands together.

Mecca just stood there staring at the man, wondering what was truly going on. Was she dead or what? At any rate, she knew he was running the show, so she just stood and waited to see what would come next.

Chapter One

So are the ways of everyone that is greedy of gain which taketh away the life of the owners thereof.

Proverbs 1:19

Brownsville, 1982

Eight-year-old Mecca Sykes lay on her stomach under her bed, frightened, crying silently, as she watched two masked men bind and gag her mother and father with duct tape around their mouths, ankles, and wrists, placing them on the living room couch. The one-bedroom project apartment smelled of dirty cat litter and cigarettes, although there wasn't an actual cat present. Mecca's wood framed bed sat in the corner of the living room opposite the couch with a dingy, sky blue, fitted sheet covering it.

Mecca was still as roaches crawled over her hands and face. She could have sworn the roaches were drinking her tears and eating the crumbs on the corners of her mouth from the bowl of Cap'n Crunch cereal she'd just finished eating. She felt them crawl into the legs and arms of her yellow pajamas, but she still didn't move. Mecca watched one of the masked men take a plastic sandwich bag filled with a grayish-colored powder out of the freezer and place it into a brown paper bag. The other masked man with the big, black revolver pointed at Mecca's parents turned to look at his partner.

"You got the shit, Darnell?" the guy holding the revolver asked. The masked man with the brown paper bag, along with Mecca's father's, eyes widened at the mention of his name.

"What the fuck is wrong with you, dude?" Darnell yelled at his partner. "Nigga, have you lost your fuckin' mind or something?"

Mecca heard her father mumbling words under the duct tape, but his words weren't audible enough for them to comprehend. The man with the brown paper bag placed it back in the refrigerator, removed his mask, and walked over to the bound couple.

"Yeah, Blast, it's me, mu'fucka. You won't be bagging this shit up for Stone no more," he shouted, spit and small pieces of food flying from his mouth and landing on Blast's face. Darnell looked in Mecca's father's eyes, and with the gun in his hand he patted his chest. "It's my turn now, nigga," he continued while Mecca's father was mumbling, shaking his head, staring at the masked men.

"God, please, let us come out of this alive. If not, look over my daughter. Let her have a life where she doesn't have to face situations like this. Please, God, I beg you. Take my daughter out of Brownsville."

Mecca's mother had tears in her eyes. She silently prayed that they would come out of this alive. She prayed for her daughter's life even if the men decided to kill her and her husband.

Mecca, by staring at her mother's face, tried to block out the fear and the roaches that crawled on her. Her mother was so pretty. She reminded Mecca of Thelma from the television show *Good Times*. Her mother looked just like Thelma and wore her black, shiny hair in a ponytail like the actress did. The only difference between Thelma and Mecca's mother was the complexion. Mecca's mother was a shade lighter than Thelma. She had a cream-colored skin tone with three black moles on her right cheekbone.

Mecca inherited her mother's complexion and features, and people often commented on her looks, playfully referring to her and her mom as twins. Mecca looked at her father and smiled. Mecca was proud to have a father who all the women in the neighborhood gawked over. He was known as Blast in Brownsville, but some called him Pretty Blast from Langston Hughes projects. With the same complexion as Mecca and her mother, Blast was a tall, muscular man with curly black hair. Everybody in Brownsville said he looked like a lighter complexioned Billy D. Williams.

Blast supported his wife and daughter by bagging up dope and stashing the dope for the neighborhood kingpin known as Stone. Blast, whose real name was Bobby Sykes, got his nickname from Stone, when in 1979, Stone stood on the corner of Mother Gaston Boulevard dressed in his usual full-length mink with diamond studded rings and necklace. When a man walked up to Stone and pointed a gun at him and told Stone to give up his stuff, Blast was coming out of the gas station on Mother Gaston and Sutter Avenue, across the street from where Stone stood.

Blast had a bottle of Crazy Horse in his hand that he couldn't wait to get home to drink. He looked at Stone from across the two, way street. Stone and his robber stood under a street light, which made the gun in the robber's hand appear to glow. It was dark outside, so the stick up man didn't notice Blast walking toward them with his black .38 Saturday Night Special. Blast nodded his head to Stone. Stone understood that Blast wanted him to run, which he did. Before the stick up man could get a shot off, Blast emptied his .38 into the man's body, leaving him dead on the corner with blood leaking from his head into the sewer. Stone ran a block up to Rockaway Avenue, where he met up with Blast.

"Damn, you blasted the shit outta that nigga. Good looking, baby!" Stone said, relieved that Blast was there to have his back. From that day, he was known as Blast. Stone put him under his wing and put him on the payroll. Knowing that about him didn't deter the two men who were there from doing what they came to do. Tired of hearing Blast mumble, Darnell took the duct tape off his mouth.

"Yo, Darnell. You ain't got to do this, homeboy. I'll tell Stone to put you on baby bro," Blast said, hoping that his life would be spared.

"Nigga, you think I was born yesterday? You think I don't know that nigga is going to try to kill me? Who the fuck you think you talking to, Blast?" Darnell laughed, and then his face turned serious quickly.

"Darnell, my word is bond! I'll make sure . . ."

"Your word is what? Oh, you think this is a game?"" Darnell said with rage on his face, pointing the gun at Blast's forehead.

Pap! Pap! Pap! Darnell put three bullets in Blast's face, sending blood and flesh flying against the beige painted wall and on Blast's wife's face and blue cotton robe. No one heard Mecca flinch and whisper her father's name. Her mother tried to break free of her restraints, but to no avail. She screamed under the duct tape, which muffled the sound.

"Oh shit, Darnell! What the fuck?" Darnell's partner barked.

"Nigga, shut the fuck up. You the reason I had to do that, and this!"

Darnell put a bullet in Mecca's mother's head. Her body slumped over onto Blast's already slumped body. Darnell grabbed the bag of heroin off the refrigerator, and looked down at the slumped bodies on the floor.

"C'mon, stupid," Darnell said, putting his gun back in his waistband.

Mecca watched both men rush out of the apartment. When the door was closed Mecca waited for a few seconds before she came out from under the bed, making sure that the men wouldn't be back forgetting something, or remembering that Blast had a daughter who looked just like him. Meanwhile, the white-robed man looked at Mecca after showing her the vision of when she was eight years old watching the murder of her parents.

***

"You didn't see then why you should have chosen a different lifestyle?" the strange man asked in an almost caring voice. Mecca could detect an undertone of sarcasm and that only pissed her off more.

"No, all I saw was my reason to make them pay! Why are you doing this? Who are you anyway?" Mecca responded angrily.

"Who I am is not important, and I'm doing this because this is my job. The question is why did you do the things you did?"

"It's all I knew," Mecca said, putting her head down, defeated. "If you're not God or whoever and you mad or if God is mad because of my life, then why did He put me in that situation? Why did He let them kill my parents? What type of God lets an eight-year-old watch her moms and pops get murdered like that? Answer that." Mecca said gravely.

"You can't blame God for the evil that men do. Those men and people like them decided on their own to do what they do. No one made you do what you did in life," the man countered. Mecca folded her arms and rolled her eyes, looking away from the man.

"Well, I was too young to comprehend or see the signs you're talking about. Whatever your name is," Mecca said sarcastically.

"Call me Lou, and I haven't finished showing you the signs you missed. I like showing you this. Your life is very interesting. You could have made a lot of money writing a book about it." Lou smiled.

Chapter Two

Thou shall not kill.
Ten Commandments

"Mommy, Daddy, get up! Please, Mommy!" Mecca crawled out from under the bed and ran to her parents. Mecca cried, shaking her parents. Both of their eyes were open with the blank stare of death in them. A look Mecca would never forget. Mecca ran to the phone that was hung up on the kitchen wall near the refrigerator. She stood on her toes to reach the phone, and dialed a seven-digit number.

"Hello."

"Aunt Ruby? My mommy and daddy gone," Mecca cried to her mother's younger sister.

"Baby, where they at?" Ruby asked tersely.

"They lying on the couch," Mecca said, sniffing and sobbing loudly. "And they won't get up, they bleeding."

Ruby instructed Mecca to open the door when the neighbor knocked. Ruby had called a friend of the family who lived on the ninth floor along with Mecca and her parents, and asked her to go check on the apartment and Mecca until she got there. It would only take her about a half an hour.

The neighbor, a girlfriend of Mecca's mother and Ruby, knocked on the door. When Mecca let her in, the woman, used to seeing murders growing up in the rough Brownsville section of Brooklyn, still reacted as if this were her first time seeing dead bodies. She covered her mouth, ran into the bathroom, and the food she ate for breakfast and lunch found its way into the roach-infested toilet. Afterward, she called the police. They arrived just as Ruby did. Ruby saw her niece sitting at the kitchen table with a plainclothes white female officer kneeled down in front of her. Mecca ran to her aunt as soon as she saw her. Mecca cried as they made contact. Ruby picked her up, and while hugging Mecca she looked at the bloodstained sheet that covered her sister's and brother-in-law's bullet-scarred bodies, not believing what took place.

"Everything is going to be okay, baby. Auntie's here," Ruby whispered in Mecca's ear as she tried to offer her some comfort. Her parents were killed right in front of her, so Ruby knew there was only so much she could say or do at the moment.

"Don't tell these cops anything, okay, baby? Don't ever speak to the cops. They are bad people! They're just like the people who did this bad thing to your mommy and daddy. Auntie gone take care of this, all right?" Ruby gave the white female cop a menacing look, whispering to Mecca as she rubbed her back.

"Uh huh," Mecca mumbled, agreeing to her aunt's wishes. Mecca whispered in her aunt's ear, "Auntie, I know who did it!"

"Tell Auntie later, okay?" Ruby whispered in Mecca's ear before putting her down on the floor.

"Is it okay if we talk to your niece?" the officer asked indistinctly, approaching them with a notepad in her hand, poised to write whatever Mecca was willing to share.

"No, it's not okay," she said. "She didn't see what happened. Her mother and father are dead, she's eight years old, and she's been through enough."

Ruby grabbed Mecca by the hand and they left the apartment. Mecca's mother's prayer was answered. Mecca left Brownsville, but her life in Brownsville was traded for another notorious Brooklyn neighborhood, Coney Island. On the drive to Coney Island in Ruby's 1982 black and yellow Camaro, Mecca informed her aunt about what she saw and heard when her parents were killed.

"Daddy talked to this guy. His name is Darnell. He's Tamika from my school brother," Mecca said in her childish tone.

"Auntie knows who you're talking about," Ruby said in a hoarse, scratchy voice. She held up two fingers to Mecca while she switched lanes on the Belt Parkway. "It was two of them?" Ruby asked.

"Yup, two of them. The other one didn't take his mask off."

Ruby nodded her head. She tried to hold back the tears because she wanted to be strong for her niece. Mecca needed her aunt, and if she saw Ruby crying, Ruby figured Mecca would be deeply affected by first the loss of her parents, and the sadness of her aunt. Ruby wiped her eyes and tried to swallow the lump in her throat. She glanced over at Mecca, who was staring out the passenger window at cars and the grimy Brooklyn neighborhoods that lay along the side of the Belt Parkway with tears running down her face. Ruby watched a roach crawl out of the collar of Mecca's pajama top. She grabbed it and smashed it in her hand.

Mecca turned and stared at her aunt as Ruby smashed the roach. They looked into each other's eyes, both understanding the silent language that Ruby would smash the people who killed her sister and brother-in-law, just like she did that roach. Without any words, Mecca continued watching the scenery through tear-blurred eyes, knowing her life from then on would never be the same.

Chapter Three

Twenty-five-year-old Ruby Davidson was the total opposite of her now deceased older sister, who Mecca was named after and was known around the way as Big M. Ruby was a dark brown, five feet eleven inches, big-boned woman. She kept her shoulder-length hair constantly wrapped with a blue bandanna, and she refused to wear women's apparel.

Ruby was a beautiful woman under the masculine mask she kept herself under. Ruby and Big M shared the same birth mother but had different fathers who neither knew. Ruby and Big M's mother was a young teenager at the ages of fifteen and sixteen when she gave birth to her two daughters. Big M's father was found dead behind a Bedford Stuyvesant bar with multiple stab wounds to his chest. His killer was never found. Ruby's father was killed in the Attica riots serving a twenty-five-to-life sentence after killing a cop walking the beat in his Brownsville neighborhood.

Ruby and Big M never met their fathers' families so there were no grandmothers or aunts or uncles they could spend weekends or holidays with. Their mother's family was spread out down south from Georgia to Louisiana, and their deep religious roots prevented them from dealing with their northern kin, who were into drugs and other sinful activities. Ruby and Mecca's mother raised her two daughters on her own until she fell victim to heroin.

One day a neighbor in Ruby and Big M's Van Dyke project building, a housing project down the block from the Langston Hughes project Mecca watched her parents get murdered in, found Ruby's mother in the staircase with a needle in her arm almost dead. The neighbor contacted the Board of Children's Welfare, also known as BCW, and informed them of what was happening in apartment 5B. The city placed Ruby and her sister in a foster home on the premise that they would be returned to their mother when she cleaned up. She never did.

Ruby, the youngest, and her year-older sister, ran away from their foster home when they were twelve and thirteen. Even though she was a year younger, Ruby was more mature than her older sister. She had more leadership qualities. It was her idea to take off from their foster home in

Queens and make their way back to Brownsville. Ruby felt like she would rather deal with the street life in which she grew up and was comfortable with, than deal with foster parents who didn't like her and her sister and only wanted them there because they were getting a check.

Ruby's body developed faster than her older sister so she looked older than her twelve years. Boys as old as eighteen approached young Ruby looking for a chance to get in her pants. Ruby had her first sexual experience on a project roof with this boy named Ron who was sixteen years old. She told her older sister afterward, revealing to her how painful it was. Ruby thought Ron was her boyfriend because he let her and her sister live in his two-bedroom apartment he shared with his ailing grandmother in the Langston Hughes projects.

He gave Ruby money and brought her clothes. The money he gave her she bought her older sister clothes with. When Ruby and her sister left the foster home, they dropped out of school. Ruby's boyfriend sold drugs in Brownsville, and eventually Ruby began to hold his drugs while he stood on the corner. He would send the customers to Ruby after the customers gave him the money.

He paid Ruby one hundred dollars a day. She saved money so one day she could get her and her sister an apartment. Mecca got a job at a local McDonalds when she turned fifteen after Ruby talked her boyfriend into taking Mecca down to get her working papers. Ron put Ruby on the lease of the apartment and when his grandmother died three years later the apartment was in her name. Ruby in turn put her sister on the lease because she had a job. Because Big M's job was a minimum-wage job, the rent would be lowered to accommodate her income.

Ron was arrested for a murder he committed against a rival clan in the Langston Hughes projects. Eventually, he pleaded to a five to fifteen-year bid and was shipped upstate to the same prison Ruby's father was killed in, Attica. Ruby was devastated.

She loved him. He was her first. She visited him faithfully. She sold the drugs he left behind and made sure his commissary account stayed in the three-digit range. She snuck in balloons of heroin for him to sell on the inside and accepted his collect calls. Ruby was always there for his calls. She wrote him love letters every night, crying herself to sleep. She never looked at another man, ignoring the advances guys made around the projects. Even some of his friends tried to get a piece of her.

"Damn, that nigga got you sucked up, girl! Let me hit it while he gone," they would say when she was seen around the projects. She ignored them all.

At the same time, her older sister was seeing a guy from the neighborhood named Bobby Sykes. The prettiest nigga Ruby ever saw. Her sister was happy and that's what made Ruby like Bobby. Ruby sometimes became jealous of her sister's relationship because her man was in jail while her sister enjoyed the company of Bobby. Bobby bought her sister anything she wanted. Her sister stayed with the latest trend of clothing and he decorated her with diamond-studded trinkets, rings, bracelets, and necklaces.

Ruby had a rough time selling dope in the projects because she was a female. At first the hustlers accepted it because they knew she was doing it to take care of her man, who they respected, but that didn't last. Ruby knew she had to get her own respect if she was going to continue to hustle. She bought a gun from an old timer who ran the neighborhood number spot. Even though it was a .25, Ruby had to make do until she was able to buy and handle a bigger one.

The day came when she had to put her weapon to use. The cousin of the guy her boyfriend had killed heard that Ruby was making money for his cousin's killer. He had to put a stop to that. He was a known troublemaker around Brownsville. Anywhere he went, something was bound to happen. He was also known to carry around a blue steel .44 Magnum and wasn't scared to use it. For that, he was given the moniker "Blue."

The rain poured down heavily on that Brownsville night, sending the dope fiends into the staircases to shoot up and the hustlers into project lobbies to hustle. Ruby stood in the hallway of her building wearing a black sheepskin with the hat to match, a black pair of Vidal Sassoon jeans, a black sweatshirt with "Ruby" written on it in white letters, and black Pumas. She had a plastic bag in her coat pocket with two bundles of dope in it, and her .25 in her other pocket.

Blue walked into the lobby with a black rain suit on with a black hooded sweatshirt underneath it. He took his hood off and glanced at Ruby while she leaned up against the silver mailboxes on the wall. He pressed the button on the elevator, acting as if he were waiting for it to come.

Ruby knew who he was. Everyone in Brownsville knew who he was. Seeing him around the way almost every day, Ruby didn't think anything of him coming into the building. She definitely didn't expect him to try to rob her as he pulled his blue steel .44 and pointed it at her chest.

Ruby had never had a gun pointed at her before and the shock of it made everything seem as if it were in slow motion. The graffiti on the walls looked as if it were moving. The pissy smell in the lobby seemed as if it were new to Ruby. She already had her hands in her pockets so she pulled out the plastic bag containing the two bundles and she put her other hand on the trigger.

"Where's the money? I know you got money. If I search you and find some I'ma blast you, bitch!" Blue said between clenched teeth.

"That's . . . that's all I got," Ruby stuttered in a fearful voice.

"Don't play with me, I know you sending that bitch-ass nigga of yours money. He lucky I wasn't around when he got my cousin or I would have murdered that punk-ass nigga!"

Hearing Blue say vulgar things about her man made all the fear in Ruby vanish. Her fear was replaced by a burning rage in her chest. With the gun still in her pocket, she pointed it at him and squeezed five times. All five shots hit Blue in his stomach, his groin, and his thighs, sending him falling face forward. His finger pulled the trigger on his gun as he fell, sending a bullet into the building's front door.

"Who's the bitch-ass nigga now, you faggot!" Ruby bent down and took his gun as he lay on the floor, moaning, then spit on him.

She ran out of the building and disappeared into the Brownsville night. A bullet had traveled to Blue's spine and he was paralyzed from the waist down. Ruby moved to Coney Island after she shot and paralyzed Blue. Blue didn't tell the cops who shot him, though. He was embarrassed by being shot by a female, let alone the girlfriend of his cousin's killer, so he told his friends that some cat he never saw before ran him down. When Ruby visited Brownsville, Blue, now being pushed around in a wheelchair by his little brother, only glanced at her, not wanting to stir up any trouble.

Ruby's world came crumbling in on her when she took one of her weekend trips to Attica to visit her boyfriend. The prison allowed inmates five visitors at one time. The prison only informed visitors that an inmate had visitors if the limit was reached; otherwise, they would allow a visitor to visit an inmate who was already on a visit. When Ruby was let in she immediately noticed her boyfriend hugging and kissing on a girl she recognized from Langston Hughes. She walked over to the couple just as they finished kissing.

"Who the fuck is this bitch, nigga?" Ruby yelled, standing between her boyfriend and the girl. Looking at the both of them, tears began to form in her eyes.

"She's a friend, Ruby. Chill out, girl," her boyfriend ex-plained, trying to grab Ruby's hand. He could tell by the look in her eyes that she was about to go off. The other visitors and inmates all watched the drama unfold. Even the correction officer positioned at a desk at the front of the visiting room watched.

"After all I been through for you, this is how you pay me back? This is what I get, you bastard?"

"Yo, you buggin', Ruby. She's my friend!"

"Friend? Fuck you mean friend, nigga? You just asked me to marry you, and I'm your friend? You better tell this bit—" the girl responded. She was shorter and smaller than Ruby, but she wasn't the least bit afraid of Ruby's stature.

She didn't get the chance to finish her sentence before Ruby was all over her. The correction officer had to intervene before total chaos broke out. He had to call for backup to get Ruby off of the girl because she was already bleeding from the nose and mouth. The visit was terminated, and Ruby left the prison distraught and heartbroken. She never visited him again. She didn't respond to his letters or accept his calls. She told her sister about the incident and the next day his name was taken off the lease. Ruby threw all of his clothes, pictures, and anything else that was his or reminded her of him in the incinerator. Ruby developed a deep hatred for men after her ordeal, and she swore to her sister that she would never let another nigga have her heart again.

As Ruby and Mecca drove the streets toward home, Ruby tried her best to get these thoughts out of her head. She couldn't help but notice how much Mecca looked like her now-deceased sister, and vowed to herself that she would do everything in her power to help Mecca get through these trying times that were clearly too much for a child to handle. Ruby also knew she couldn't dwell on the past, and had to keep the flow going in her own life.

Ruby brought her niece to her Coney Island apartment a few blocks away from the amusement park the neighborhood was famous for. Her duplex apartment on Twenty-fourth Street between Surf and Mermaid Avenues was decorated with mirrored walls and bright-colored furniture. It had a seventies look to it. Ruby was living in the apartment with a female companion, but she was currently serving a ten-year sentence for possession of a half kilo of heroin found in a backpack she attempted to bring on a Greyhound bus headed to Virginia. When they entered the apartment, Ruby turned on the television for Mecca to watch.

"You hungry, baby?" she asked while walking into the kitchen. Ruby didn't know why she asked that question, knowing her niece's appetite probably was gone by what she had seen. She didn't have an appetite herself. She just wanted to take Mecca's mind off of what had happened as much as she could.

"Yes, Auntie, do you have Cap'n Crunch?" Mecca replied to her surprise. Ruby knew at that moment that Mecca was tougher than the average girl her age. If she could get through the death of her parents with no problem, anything else that would come her way would be a breeze.

Chapter Four

He that killeth with the sword must
be killed with the sword.
Revelations 13:10

After two weeks of taking Mecca shopping for new clothes and furniture for the room once used by Ruby's roommate, Mecca returned to school. Ruby allowed Mecca to continue to attend school in Brownsville with all of her friends. She, along with some of Mecca's teachers, noticed a change in Mecca's attitude immediately. Her temper, to be exact.

Her first explosion was directed toward a girl her age named Tamika, the sister of her parents' killer. Tamika didn't know it was her brother who had killed Mecca's parents. Tamika hardly saw her brother, and when he did come home it would be after a week of him missing and he would come home while Tamika was asleep. When she got home from school, he would be gone. It all popped off when Tamika asked Mecca for some candy during lunch period, something she was better off leaving alone.

"Can I get one of your Now and Laters?"

"No! Get your own," Mecca replied to Tamika while rolling her eyes.

"Forget you then," Tamika came back, sucking her teeth and rolling her eyes at Mecca. When she turned to walk away she didn't see Mecca charging at her like a speeding train. By the time she turned around, hearing the footsteps coming toward her, Mecca was swinging wildly, punching and scratching Tamika's face. She pulled Tamika's hair, forcing her to the floor and causing Tamika to squeal in pain.

"Mecca, get off me! You're hurting me!"

Mecca had rage in her eyes and she didn't hear Tamika's cry. She didn't hear the other students laughing and screaming for Mecca to "beat her up!" and "stop, Mecca, you're hurting her!"

Teachers heard the commotion and went to break it up. When Mecca was pulled off of Tamika, she had patches of her hair missing. Her face was scratched and bruised. Mecca was breathing hard and just stared at Tamika while the teachers walked her to the principal's office, where Mecca was told she was on a three-day suspension. Mecca thought she would come home to an angry Ruby. Instead, Ruby waited for Mecca to return home to a diamond bracelet and brand new Sergio Valente jeans and Reebok sneakers. Ruby was usually high off of the weed she constantly smoked, and smiled at Mecca.

"You beat that li'l bitch ass, Mecca?"

"Yeah, Auntie, I beat her ass." Mecca smiled back at her aunt.

Ruby hugged her niece and said, "If anybody says something you don't like or tries to hurt your feelings, you beat they ass. If they beat you, you grab a bottle, a knife, anything you can find and you make sure they feel pain, you hear me?" Ruby asked. With a serious look on her face, she held Mecca's shoulders and continued, "If I ever hear you let somebody hit you and you ain't do nothing, I'll beat your ass myself."

Ruby smiled again and handed Mecca her gifts. When teachers complained to Ruby, she told them she would deal with Mecca. Eventually Mecca got expelled at numerous schools in Brooklyn. By the time she reached junior high, Mecca had been to six elementary schools, and ended up in a school for problem kids known as "six hundred schools."

Ruby sold dope out of the apartment and didn't have to worry about standing on corners subjected to harassing beat cops and detectives and the stick up kids. Coney Island was full of stick up kids. Ruby had regular clientele. People she knew. She didn't run a spot where just anyone could come cop; her customers were also friends she invited in to drink and gossip with, most of them women.

Ruby had some of the same customers she had before leaving Brownsville, and it was from her Brownsville customers that she received info she needed about the goings-on in Brownsville. The who's who and what's what of the neighborhood. This is how Ruby received the information she needed to make her move against the man responsible for killing her sister and her brother-in-law, and making her niece an orphan.

The kids in Mecca's new Coney Island neighborhood learned the hard way that Mecca wasn't the social type. Ruby kept Mecca's hair tightly corn-rowed, which made Mecca's eyes seem catlike. The look in Mecca's light brown eyes scared a lot of the kids. A lot of the kids envied Mecca, due to Ruby making sure that Mecca's clothes were of the latest fashion. Mecca wore clothes that kids in Coney Island wouldn't see until months later and wouldn't be able to have because their parents couldn't afford them.

What Mecca didn't know was that her clothes were from boosters that Ruby paid for with dope or were given to her by her friends. The only things Ruby bought for Mecca were jewelry, sneakers, and shoes. Mecca wore two-karat diamond earrings, diamond-flooded wrist and ankle bracelets, and she had every cartridge for the Atari 2600 and the 3200 ever made.

When the summer of 1983 rolled in, Mecca met a girl her age named Dawn who lived down the hall from her tenth floor apartment. Dawn's mother was one of Ruby's customers and asked Ruby if Dawn could stay at her apartment while she went out on "dates," which everybody in Coney Island knew were Johns. She sold her body to support her habit. At first, Mecca hated the dark-skinned, thick, bushy-haired girl. Dawn wore dirty clothes, smelled like piss, and she was always ashy. Mecca didn't like her out of jealousy. Ruby started giving Dawn new clothes; she bathed Dawn, and did her hair the same way she did Mecca's.

Mecca found her excuse to try to physically hurt Dawn when Dawn tried to steal one of Mecca's Atari cartridges. They were playing each other in a game of Frogger when Mecca noticed out of the corner of her eye the print of a cartridge in Dawn's dungaree pockets. Mecca dropped her joystick and went to grab Dawns pocket.

"What are you doing?" Dawn jumped back and yelled.

Mecca gave her the look that usually scared other kids away from her, but to her surprise Dawn returned the look. Mecca was caught off guard. She was not used to anyone not being scared when she gave them that menacing stare.

"Gimme my cartridge, you thief!" Mecca barked.

"This ain't yours!" Dawn grabbed her pocket when she saw Mecca stare at it.

"Yes, it is!" Mecca yelled, charging at Dawn, who was no pushover.

This was no easy fight for Mecca. Dawn was just as strong and ferocious as she was. Ruby, in her bedroom, was bagging up heroin into small, white packets, wearing a hospital mask over her face as not to inhale the fumes, when she heard the argument going on between the girls, and ran out to see what the commotion was. When she entered the living room she saw Mecca and Dawn both with ripped T-shirts, hair out wild, and both had scratches and blood coming out of their noses. They were both out of breath holding each other's hair, and swinging their arms at each other. Ruby watched them fight for a few more minutes, grinning, then when she realized they had both had enough, she stepped between them, holding them apart from each other.

"All right, you two! Y'all know damn well y'all had enough. I don't know what y'all was fighting for. . . ."

"She tried to—" Mecca replied, pointing to Dawn, out of breath.

Ruby cut her off. "I don't want to know. The way y'all fought each other y'all better off being friends and holding each other down against them people that's going to hate you for who you are. Whatever it was, don't let it come between y'all again. Don't let nothing come between y'all, I want y'all to be like sisters, you hear me?"

Both girls stared at each other, neither not wanting to fight each other again. Mecca had to admit to herself Dawn was tough and Dawn thought the same of Mecca. Dawn also thought Mecca was a spoiled brat who was spoon-fed and didn't have to fight for anything, but she had a change of heart after the fight Mecca had put up.

"I said did y'all hear me?" Ruby grumbled. Both girls nodded their heads.

Dawn never tried to take anything from Mecca again. In fact, she stole cartridges from other kids that Mecca didn't have, and gave them to her. Afterward, Mecca started to like Dawn, and when Mecca realized Dawn's mother was a fiend she felt sorry for Dawn and their bond got tighter. Ruby enrolled Dawn in the same school as Mecca and the two became inseparable. When you fought one, you fought the other. Eventually no one messed with the two girls. Kids in their Brownsville school started calling them The Devil's Daughters.

The man in the white robe laughed loudly while Mecca just stared. "The Devil's Daughters!" the white-robed man called Lou yelled, chuckling.

"I didn't tell anybody to call us that. So what's so funny?" Mecca asked with anger in her voice.

Lou stopped laughing and said, "I know you didn't tell no one to call y'all that. It's what they saw in you and her. People see you better than you see yourself, Mecca. That's why now I'm giving you the opportunity to see yourself from day one and the people around you, I'm giving you the opportunity to see how your life affected others and how people saw you."

"I don't care how people saw me," Mecca said sternly.

"After this, you're going to wish you had cared, Ms. Mecca."

Chapter Five

For by means of a whorish woman a man is brought to a piece of bread and the adulteress will hunt for the precious life.

Proverbs 6:26

The Summer of 1987

The summer of 1987 was one of the best summers Ruby ever had. Crack was on the scene and Ruby became acquainted with the rock form of cocaine, and established a relationship with it that fattened her pockets. The Langston Hughes projects were full of crack fiends looking for the dealer who had the best stuff. A lot of good people fell victim to the lure of the three-minute high that crack gave.

A lot of people Ruby knew from her younger days were now strung out, people who were once a part of the in crowd. The people who everyone in the hood wanted to be like, dress like, and talk like got bit by the crack epidemic, even Stone.

When Stone, the once kingpin of the projects became a full-fledged crack-head, he eventually lost the respect of his soldiers and confidants. He started smoking his own product until he went broke. Darnell, the man who killed Ruby's sister and brother-in-law, made his move. He had the product and the product was good. With that came the soldiers. Stone's ex-soldiers. In no time Darnell was the biggest cat in the projects. Ruby set up shop in Coney Island, and she had her friend Monique sell her stuff in Langston Hughes. Ruby wasn't making as much as Darnell was, but it was enough. Most of her money was being made on her Coney Island block.

"Girl, guess who home?" Monique asked as if she was about to deliver bad news.

"Who?" Ruby asked while she chopped up a rock the size of a tennis ball on a white china dish with a razor blade. She placed the pebbles inside small vials with yellow tops.

"Your ex-nigga a Five Percenter now. They call him Wise, like the dumb nigga wise or something," Monique giggled.

Monique was the only person Ruby talked to about the ordeal with Wise. Monique and Ruby had been friends since they were kids growing up in Brownsville. Ruby talked to Monique about men because Monique was an expert when it came to dealing with the opposite sex. She had men wrapped around her finger. Her voluptuous body and striking good looks were the keys to making men bow at her feet. She had a caramel complexion and hazel eyes with firm C-cup breasts. Monique had an exotic look having been born to a Panamanian mother and Cuban father. Oddly, Monique didn't know a lick of Spanish.

The thought of seeing her ex made Ruby nervous. She wondered how she would react or feel when she saw him. She wondered how he looked. Was he buff from lifting weights in jail? Did he still look the same with his fine self? His curly hair that looked wet, his chinky eyes, and those dimples . . . damn.

"Girl, what you thinking about?" Monique asked, snapping Ruby out of her daydream.

"I was thinking how much product I left in Coney Island," Ruby lied. Monique knew she was lying, also. She knew her girl and knew when she was hurt, happy, and lying.

"Please, Ruby, you thinking about that clown Wise or whatever he call himself." Monique laughed at Ruby's expense, causing Ruby to laugh too.

"You know me too good. I got to change my ways."

"What's there to think about? That nigga old news," Monique said, hoping Ruby wasn't thinking about reconciling her and Wise's relationship. She knew how hurt Ruby was when she had gone on that visit and saw him hugging and kissing another woman. She didn't want her best friend to go through that again. People just didn't know how much Ruby changed after that episode.

"You right, girl. Fuck that clown," Ruby said, continuing to chop on the crack rock she had on the plate. "It's about money and you know what m-o-n-e-y means to us!"

In unison, Ruby and Monique yelled, "Money Over Niggas Every Year!" They both howled in laughter.

Mecca was now thirteen years old and still a virgin. Her body developed quickly. The boys in her junior high school noticed the feisty thirteen-year-old, and her friend, Dawn, who had also developed quickly.

Dawn had already lost her virginity in the school bathroom to a Puerto Rican boy in her social studies class. They started off passing notes to each other, then Dawn answered the last letter with a check in the "yes" box when he asked if she wanted to go out with him. He motioned for her to meet him when the bell rang to change classes. They snuck to the basement and had sex in the bathroom.

"Did you like it?" Mecca asked curiously.

"At first I didn't, because it hurt. Then it started feeling good," Dawn replied shyly.

"You so nasty." Mecca smiled and playfully hit Dawn on the shoulder.

Dawn sucked her teeth. "Please, you better get you some before your stuff dry up and die."

Both girls laughed. Mecca and Dawn had to gain their respect back when they entered junior high. Their reputations stayed intact the entire time. Both Mecca and Dawn were problem students, so they both had to attend the "six hundred school" for bad kids. Ruby thought Mecca would be cool going to school in Brownsville because that's where her friends were, and when she had tried to school Mecca in her Coney Island neighborhood she kept getting into fights. The sad thing was, the fights continued in Brownsville. It was a new school and there were new foes at the time, and some of the kids from their elementary schools were there and spread the word that Dawn and Mecca were not to be fucked with. But with some people, examples had to me made.

The opportunity presented itself when the girlfriend of a guy who had a crush on Mecca found out that he liked her. Instead of confronting her boyfriend, she chose to approach Mecca, who didn't even know the boy. The girl made a bad choice. A choice that she had to carry for the rest of her life.

Dawn and Mecca both dressed in tight-fitting Lee Jeans. Mecca with burgundy pinstriped ones with burgundy on white shell-top Adidas, and a white sweat shirt with "Mecca" written in script on the upper left corner, and giant door knocker earrings. Dawn wore black ones with black on white shell-top Adidas, and a white sweatshirt with matching earrings. They both walked down the crowded hallway heading toward the exit, when a light-skinned girl with a short Jherri curl that left stains on her no-name brand, button-down blue shirt approached Mecca with an angry look on her face.

"You better stay away from my man!"

Mecca and Dawn looked at each other, then back at the girl, confused. "Who you talking to?" Mecca asked.

"I'm talking to you! Stay away from Tah or I'm gonna . . ." the girl replied, stepping closer to Mecca's face.

Mecca didn't give her the opportunity to finish her threat. She was punching the girl in the face and pulled her Jherri curl, pulling the girl down to the floor. Dawn started kicking the girl in the stomach and the face. The girl screamed as the crowd in the hallway gathered around, watching the two fly girls beat up the girl who had approached them with hostility. While the girl was down, she managed to look up and spit in Mecca's face. Mecca turned as red as an apple. Mecca reached in her back pocket and pulled out a Gem Star razor that she had found on the kitchen table. Ruby used them to chop up her drugs.

Grabbing the girl by the back of her head, holding her hair, she sliced the girl's face from her ear to the corner of her lip. The blood squirted from the girl's face. She tried to hold her face closed so the blood wouldn't leak out.

"She cut me! Get this bitch off of me!"

When the crowd saw all the blood, they started walking away. Mecca and Dawn both ran to the exit and rushed to the bus stop to catch the bus heading home. Later that day, two cops knocked on Monique's door in Langston Hughes looking for Dawn and Mecca. The girls used Monique's address so they could go to school in Brownsville. They had to live in the zone in order to attend the school. If the school found out they lived in Coney Island, they wouldn't be allowed to attend. The cops told Monique that they had a warrant for the arrest of Dawn and Mecca. Monique informed both of them that Dawn and Mecca didn't return home that day. When they did she would bring them to the station. She lied.

"Who the hell is Tah, Dawn?" Mecca asked Dawn while they rode the bus home.

"You know him by face. He's in my math class," Dawn replied, looking out the window while the bus rode through the Pitkin Avenue shopping area.

"How he look? He better be cute after all this bullshit we going through," Mecca said.

"He all right. He ain't no LL Cool J. He gets fresh and all that. He pump jums in Brownsville houses."

"You know we can't go back to school, right?" Mecca said more than asked.

Dawn sighed. "Yeah, I know. Fuck it, I'm tired of school anyway. I'm ready to start making some dough."

"What are you talking about, Dawn?" Mecca asked with a look on her face that said, "I know you ain't talking about what I think you're talking about."

"I'm talking about the way your aunt gets money. Like everybody else. I'm tired of taking handouts from Ruby, Mecca. I'm ready to get down with the program."

Mecca shook her head at her friend. *Dawn is going crazy*, she thought. It's probably losing her virginity that messed her brain up. Mecca hoped Dawn was just talking and not dead serious about it.

"Dawn, you crazy, girl," was all she could say before riding the rest of the way to Coney Island in silence.

The white-robed man named Lou folded his arms and stared at Mecca for a few seconds.

"What?" Mecca asked tersely.

"Did that girl deserve to have her face sliced up like that?"

Mecca sucked her teeth and looked away from Lou. "Shoot, she spit on me. I ain't letting nobody spit on me, for real."

"Don't you see how reckless you were, Mecca? I could under-stand you being young and in emotional pain from the tragic loss of your parents, but to live your life blaming everybody for it? It's not fair, Mecca. Two people are responsible for what happened to your parents. Not the eight million people that live in New York City."

"What do you care? It wasn't your family!" Mecca barked. "You don't know what it feels like. How you going to tell me how I should have felt?"

"I didn't tell you how you should feel. I'm just saying you should have learned how to deal with your feelings better than the way you did," Lou shot back.

"What's the point then?" Mecca asked, lifting her hands in a protesting manner while shrugging her shoulders

"I haven't gotten to that yet. When I do you'll be the first to know."

Chapter Six

His mischief shall return upon his own head, and his violent dealing shall come down upon his own plate.

Psalms 7:18

"Damn, Stone. How you let yourself go like that, man? This ain't you, man!" Wise said as he and Stone stood on the corner of Rockaway Avenue and Dumont in Tilden Projects.

It was a hot, sunny day. There were people barbecuing all around the projects. Hustlers in fancy cars drove up and down Rockaway Avenue while corner hustlers stared in envy. Women in Daisy Dukes and T-shirts tied in knots exposing belly buttons with large, gold earrings in their ears waved to the hustlers, looking for attention from them and hopefully a chance to ride in their car.

Kids played in fire hydrants while some kids pointed at passing cars screaming to each other, "That's my car!" and "Punch buggy got my license!"

Stone, dressed in a dirty, blue suede–front jacket with holes in it and ripped-up jeans and dirty, red suede Pumas, looked down while his mouth twitched, looking for an answer to Wise's question.

"I'll be back on my feet in no time, kid! Watch, ain't nothing change, baby." Stone smiled, showing yellow-stained teeth with some missing. His skin was ashy and dull, and though he was in his late thirties he looked to be in his fifties.

Wise looked at Stone, disgusted. This was a man Wise had looked up to when he was younger. This was his idol. Stone had it all. The women. The big caddies. Diamond-studded jewels and name belts. He wore the flyest clothes money could buy. Minks, silk suits, gators, crocs, and other reptiles on his feet. He was a legend. He was a stone cold killer everyone looked up to. Now, look at him.

"So what's going on around here, Stone? Who's doing what?"

Wise wore a bright red BVD nylon T-shirt, showing his muscular build from years of working out in prison. His black Calvin Klein jeans matched his black Reebok Classics. His once curly hair was now cut low with 360 waves.

"You know Darnell from the projects got things sowed up over there. Boy blew up something decent," Stone said in admiration.

"Word?" Wise asked, nodding his head.

"The only person besides Darnell getting some money is your girl Ruby. She doing okay for herself." Stone continued rocking back and forth on one leg at a time.

The mention of Ruby's name brought back memories for Wise. He also still felt the same guilt he felt for years after being caught on the visiting floor with a girl who was actually a mule bringing up weed and dope for him to sell. The kiss was the girl passing him dope. He led the girl on to thinking they were in a relationship because she wouldn't do what she was asked if he didn't give her the attention she wanted.

He didn't need her to do it because Ruby was doing it for him. His greed got the best of him, though. He never stopped loving Ruby; he dreamed of her every night for the four years he did time. He secretly cried in his cell when he didn't hear from her. When she wrote her last letter, it tore Wise up inside. The letter was stamped in his mind forever.

Dear backstabbing motherfucker,

I guess you wanted your cake and you wanted to eat it, too. I hope that bitch is worth losing someone who would have walked through hell with you. All the risk I took to make your bid comfortable and this is what I get? You a selfish bastard and you know what? I don't hate you for this. I'm bigger than that. It's a learning experience for me. I learned you ain't shit and you never gonna be shit. I hope you have a happy marriage. From someone who used to worship the ground you walked on.

Bye Forever!

Wise vowed to prove to Ruby that he was a better person than she thought he was. He vowed that he would make it up to her and try to win her heart back. When he began studying under the teaching of the Five Percent Nation, he had a different outlook on women. They were queens of civilization, goddesses of the universe. A man couldn't be a complete man without a woman who represented wisdom. The man represented knowledge and with knowledge and wisdom comes understanding, which represents the child. Wise needed a queen and he wanted that queen to be Ruby. What Wise didn't understand was a woman. He didn't understand a woman scorned. When she's done with you, she's done.

"That girl ain't nothing to fuck with, baby bro. She got her thing mapped out. She takes care of business, you hear me?" Stone said, while Wise was in deep thought on how he would win Ruby's heart back.

"I hear you, man," Wise replied.

"Speaking of the devil," Stone said excitedly, pointing toward Ruby walking toward them. "There she goes now!"

Both Ruby's and Wise's hearts beat fast as they caught eye contact with each other. It was like Ruby was walking in slow motion when he looked at her. Dressed in a tight, blue Calvin Klein jeans set that showed her thick thighs and bulging hips, which left no doubt about the size of her ass, her bootie socks had a black stripe on the rim matching her black and white Diadoras. Her rope chain was the size of a small child's arm. As usual, she wore her hair in a black bandanna scarf, this time with thick "baby hair" showing out of the front of it.

Ruby had to make a stop in the building Stone and Wise stood in front of. It was just a coincidence that she would run into him in another project only a few blocks from Langston Hughes. Ruby had customers in Tilden projects so her face was a regular around there.

Noticing him, Ruby became nervous, with perspiration beginning to cover her palms. It was just the way she imagined. He would come home buffed and beautiful and ready to fuck some woman's brains out with all those years backed up in him. He had the glow guys have when they come home from the penitentiary. His hair was sharply shaped up and his waves did a perfect circle around his head. His arms bulged and his chest muscles showed through his shirt. Ruby's mouth turned dry and she felt her body shaking as she came face to face with him. Wise smiled, showing pearly white teeth.

"Ruby, what's up, girl?" he asked while reaching out to hug her.

Ruby didn't hug him, but she let him embrace her. She felt the hardness of his body and her pussy began to throb. When she didn't return the hug, Wise backed up and looked at her with a questionable look.

"It's like that?"

"How you doing, Ron?" Ruby asked, using his birth name purposely.

"My name is Wise now. Please don't use my government name."

Ruby already knew he was calling himself Wise. She purposely called him that to irritate him. She held her grudge, something he would find out the hard way.

"What's up, Stone?" she asked, smiling at Stone, then return-ing to the serious look when she looked back at Wise. "It was nice seeing you, Ron, I mean, Wise. Welcome home," Ruby said, walking toward the entrance of the high-rise building.

Wise grabbed her hand and tried to pull her toward him. "Ruby, can I talk to you for a minute?"

Ruby, rolled her eyes. "I got something important to take care of. Time is money and my time is valuable, something you didn't realize a few years ago."

"Ruby, how many times do I have to apologize for what I did? I told you she was a mule. I had to act like I liked her so she would keep bringing my shit up north," he pleaded.

"I wasn't mule enough for you?" Ruby asked. "Listen, Wise, that's old shit. Like our relationship is. Good to see you home, have a good life. I'm too old to be carrying on about this. So what is it that you want to say to me?"

Stone was right, Wise thought. She definitely changed. *She's colder than she was before.* Ruby always had a good heart and she was loyal to those she loved. Her heart was no longer warm, and she had a look in her eyes that said, "Don't fuck with me."

"I heard you getting money pushing rock," Wise said. Ruby cut her eyes at Stone who was still rocking his body, acting as if he wasn't paying attention to the conversation. "I wanna help you expand, lock all this shit down around here."

"And how do you plan on doing that?" she asked skeptically. Ruby faced him with her arms folded.

Wise looked at Stone from the corner of his eye then back at Ruby. "I can't discuss that here. Can I take you to get some-thing to eat later on?" he asked.

I can't let him do this to me. He's trying to sneak back into my life. Once a dog, always a dog. He'll only hurt me and I won't let another man do this to me, Ruby thought.

Ruby's dealing with men had drastically changed since the day she found Wise kissing another woman on the prison visiting floor. It took her a year to even entertain her desire to have sex with a man, and when she did, it was hit and run. Mecca found out how drastic the change was on one of her numerous suspensions from school; she walked in on Monique's face deep between Ruby's legs. Monique was doing such a good job that Ruby didn't even notice Mecca walk in the house. Ruby lay on the couch with her eyes closed, holding Monique's head. Both women were stark naked.

"Meet me in Langston Hughes at seven-thirty," Ruby said to Wise.

She walked away thinking, *I won't let him back in my heart, but he could be of good use for the plan I got. When I'm done with what I got to do, then I'll be rid of his no- good ass. Let another woman go through the heartache that these niggas come with.*

Wise turned to Stone, who looked at him with a look that spelled pitiful.

"Never let a once a month–bleeding bitch think that you need her. She'll do nothing but play on it," Stone said.

Wise shook his head. "See, that's why you're in the position you're in. You can't see ahead. You can't see the big picture. Sometimes, you gotta fake it to make it, baby." Wise grinned.

Wise knocked on Monique's door at seven-thirty on the dot. Ruby answered the door and thought, *Damn, this nigga really look good.*

Inside the apartment, Rakim's "I Ain't No Joke" blasted out of the speakers. Ruby wore a pair of acid wash jeans by Calvin Klein with the matching jean jacket. She had gotten rid of the low cut years ago and wore her hair in a ponytail with bangs in the front. On her feet she had a pair of white and green Gucci sneakers. Wise took Ruby to Juniors restaurant in downtown Brooklyn before this meeting. He told her his plan to take over Brownsville.

"What you going to do about Darnell? He got things locked," Ruby asked as they sat at a table in the crowded restaurant.

"Once I get Tilden locked, I'ma move on Van Dyke projects. By then I'll be ready for Darnell," Wise replied. "For now I need to get product. I need a connect, and I heard your shit is good shit."

Ruby knew Wise had something up his sleeve. He wanted her connect. He didn't even have any soldiers to set up in Tilden and Van Dyke. Those niggas over there wouldn't be trying to hear that shit. Wise just came home thinking this was 1982. *These niggas is playing with guns now.* Ruby listened to Wise ramble on and on. Ruby leaned over the table to get close to Wise's face. He leaned in, thinking she wanted to kiss him.

"Nigga, you got toast?" she asked, trying to call his bluff. Wise leaned back, surprised that Ruby was on top of her game like that.

"Not yet. You know anybody who got some?"

Ruby sighed, then answered, "I got a better plan. You can get rid of Darnell quicker than your plan. Come see me tomorrow."

Wise walked Ruby to Monique's door. Ruby knew he hadn't asked her out to try to start over. He wanted to use her to get to her connect. *That nigga ain't change. He's even worse than he was before he went in, a selfish nigga with plans to get rich by stepping on toes. What niggas in jail don't realize is that times change and people do too. They think things are supposed to be the way they were before they went in. This is why a lot of cats come home and get killed.*

Wise set up a meeting with Darnell on the pretense that Wise knew of a heist where the score would be twenty or more kilos of cocaine. Even though Darnell was doing good pushing dope and crack, grossing ten kilos of cocaine and three of heroin, he would still participate in a heist. It was in him. That's how he got in the position he was in now. Selling drugs made him hood rich, but robbery was his first love. It's the Brownsville way.

Wise had Darnell meet him at Monique's apartment. He showed up in style just to show Wise that he was the man in Brownsville. Darnell loved to show off. He always wanted to be like Stone. Darnell wore a four-finger ring with his name in diamonds. He wore diamond-flooded name buckles with a large diamond in one ear. He entered Monique's apartment wearing a leather blazer with a black turtleneck, and a big rope chain with a medallion the size of a small china plate. His name was on the medallion flooded with diamonds, and he had on black Levi jeans and black-on-white Nike Cortezas.

"Peace, God," Wise said to Darnell. Darnell was also a Five Percenter, which made him willing to meet with Wise without being skeptical about it. Wise told him of the heist in the lingo of the Five Percenters.

"Yo, God. One of the gods I was in Comstock with built with me about this eighty-fiver who's making a lot of Divine Cipher Equality. He said this cat is sex. He lives in Mecca in Grant projects. We can get era," Wise said to Darnell, telling him that a non-believer he met in prison was getting mad dough but he was soft. He wanted Darnell to know that getting his money would be a piece of cake. Darnell agreed to meet with Wise to plan it.

"You want something to drink, God?" Wise asked. "I just got some Old E."

"Yeah. It's cold?" Darnell asked, sitting at the kitchen table, taking his blazer off and placing it on the back of the chair.

Wise got up from the table. "Why equal self?" he said, meaning "yes" in the coded language of Five Percenters. He went to the refrigerator and poured beer in milk glasses. After giving Darnell his drink, Wise sat down at the table across from Darnell.

"How much this cat got in the crib?" Darnell asked.

"The bitch said wisdom cipher or more," Wise answered, meaning twenty or more.

"She supposed to call you in an hour, right?" Darnell asked, drinking the beer.

"Yeah, she said as soon as this cat call and tell her he on the way. That's how he do, so the broad could tell him if it's clear for him to come through. Real cautious nigga."

"What you plan on doing with the coke?" Darnell asked Wise curiously.

"I was hoping I could team up with you and we could take over the whole villa. Tilden, Brownsville Houses, Sethlow, and Van Dyke. We'll be billionaires, God!" Wise said, but what he was really thinking was that Darnell was a dumb-ass nigga. *Ain't no coke. The coke that he'll get is going to be Ruby's, and once I get close to her connect, I plan to get her out the way, too.*

This nigga think he going to be alive after this heist, he got another think coming. I'ma blow this nigga head off. Who the fuck he think he is? He do a little bid and think he's going to come home and get rich in my hood? Darnell smiled.

"It sounds good. Yeah, God, we'll be dumb rich."

After a half hour, Darnell began to get real tired. His speech started to slur and his eyes got heavy. He shook his head, trying to wake himself up.

"Damn, a nigga feel real crazy fucking with that beer."

Wise watched as his eyes began to shut. The sleeping pills Ruby gave him were powerful. He put more in the beer than what Ruby had told him. *"Put three in. He'll be knocked out for hours. If you put too much, nigga fuck around and die."* Wise put in six.

Darnell fell out of the chair and passed out on the kitchen floor. Ruby, dressed in a green velour Nike suit from Dapper Dan, and Monique, dressed in the same suit but in white with green trimming around the word Nike on her chest, came out of the bathroom after sitting in it for an hour. What Wise didn't know was that both women were armed with black 9 mm Berettas equipped with silencers.

"I got Darnell, take care of Dumb," Ruby whispered, calling Wise the name she and Monique jokingly called him.

"Search his pockets" Wise said to both women, walking to the bathroom. "I gotta take a piss."

When Wise closed the bathroom door, Ruby whispered to Monique, "Mo, open the window right there." Ruby pointed to the kitchen window.

While Monique opened the window, Ruby dragged Darnell's limp body to it. Monique looked at Ruby, confused.

"What you doing, Ruby?" she whispered with confusion written over her face.

"Grab his legs. I'm throwing him out of the window."

Monique shook her head while grabbing Darnell by his feet. Monique thought that Ruby was really insane. She'd be damned if she ever crossed her.

Both women shoved Darnell's body out of the window, letting it drop nine stories to his death. People sitting around and walking around the projects heard a loud thump, then turned to see Darnell's body slam head first into the cement and watched his brain pop out of his head. Women screamed and guys around the projects gaped at seeing their boss, friend, and some enemies to Darnell, splattered on the concrete.

When Wise came out of the bathroom, Ruby stood in front of the bathroom door as he came out. Ruby put her finger to her mouth, gesturing for Wise to say nothing. "We gotta get out of here," she whispered.

"Where's Darnell?" Wise asked, trying to look around Ruby's shoulder.

"We threw him out of the window," Ruby replied.

"Y'all did what?" he yelled, pushing Ruby out of the way. "Y'all bitches is crazy! We were supposed to tie him up! Then when he woke up make him take us to his stash!" Wise said. Wise walked to the door, pissed that the plan had somehow changed. "I'm outta here! Y'all bitches is stupid!"

Ruby and Monique followed him out the door. In the piss-smelling hallway you could hear Slick Rick and Doug E. Fresh's "The Show" blasting from someone's apartment.

Wise mumbled all the way to the elevator. He changed his mind, walking to the staircase with Ruby and Monique in tow. When they entered the graffiti-covered stairs, Monique and Ruby pulled out their silencer-equipped 9 mm, and as Wise descended, they both pumped bullets into his back and the back of his head.

As his body rolled down the stairs, Ruby stood on top of him and emptied the clip in him. Ruby didn't hear the footsteps coming up the stairs, and she couldn't see behind the walled staircase.

When Mecca came around the landing, she almost stepped on Wise's body. Mecca jumped back in shock, and then looked up at Ruby and Monique, both with guns in their hands.

"Mecca, where are you coming from?" Ruby whispered.

Mecca looked at Wise, then back at Ruby, barely able to speak. "The . . . the elevator is broke."

"You didn't see where that life was headed then Mecca?" Lou stared at Mecca, shrugging his shoulders with his hands up.

"That had nothing to do with me." Mecca snorted.

"I didn't say it did, but you saw the evil that's attributed to the lifestyle. After that, why didn't you see it wasn't worth it?"

"What other choices did I have? My aunt was everything to me. She was what I wanted to be. It was all I knew!" Mecca cried.

"I doubt that, Mecca. There were people in your life who didn't live like that. There were people who wanted better for you. You turned your back on those people," Lou said.

"Who? What people? I don't remember anybody trying to change me. Most people I knew either was in the game and the ones that weren't had they hands out for money for things they didn't have," Mecca countered.

Lou shook his head. "That's why I'm here. You have a bad memory, Mecca. So I'll remind you."

Chapter Seven

Many waters cannot quench love; neither can the floods drown it.

Songs of Solomon 8:7

By the time 1990 came around, Mecca and Dawn were knee-deep in the drug game. They gave Ruby's workers the packages of crack and collected the money. Dawn managed the spots in Coney Island while Mecca managed the spots in Brownsville.

Ruby had spots in each project in Brownsville. Each spot was making over $20,000 a day, and she paid the workers $2,000 a week. She put Stone in a rehab program with a promise to put him back on his feet if he completed it. When he completed the program, Stone made sure each spot ran smoothly. He was security, and Ruby paid him the same she paid Mecca and Dawn.

The spot in the Brownsville Houses was having problems with a local stick up crew headed by a guy named Tah. When Mecca was told about it from the workers, she remembered the name from somewhere but couldn't put a face to it. When she informed Ruby, Ruby barked, "What the fuck do I pay Stone for? And what's up with those punk-ass workers? None of them got crons?"

Mecca told Stone about the stick up crew and all he said was "I'll handle it." He never did. Word on the street was that Stone got soft and the young cats lost respect for him. Tah and the stick up crew took advantage of the word about Stone going soft and stuck him up at a block party in Brownsville houses.

"If I gotta go to them projects myself and handle these clowns, I'll fuck around and kill them niggas, then I'll kill Stone's punk ass!" Ruby growled.

Ruby stayed away from Brownsville as much as possible. The gritty section of Brooklyn was too unpredictable for her. Stick up kids and killers were born and raised on the Brownsville streets every day, and she didn't want to be some young hot head's first of many bodies. When she did show up in Brownsville in her ocean green Sterling with BBS rims, it was usually in the early morning hours to see Stone and to remind the residents of Brownsville that she was still around, and she wasn't hiding in the villa she bought in the Hamptons where she and Monique now stayed.

Ruby and Monique had become full-fledged lesbian lovers. Monique treated Mecca like a daughter. She loved Mecca as if she were her daughter, and she became concerned with Mecca being on the street. After a lovemaking session with Ruby, Monique expressed her concern as they lay naked on their king-sized, heart shaped waterbed with red satin sheets and pillows.

"Ruby, them streets are dangerous. You shouldn't have Mecca out there. She needs to get herself a job or something or finish school. Niggas don't care if she a girl or not, they'll treat her just like a nigga when it comes to that money. She still damn near a baby."

Ruby folded her arms under her head and sighed. "She's young, but she got a old soul. Mecca knows how to handle herself." Ruby looked over at Monique and continued. "Monique, you know that girl ain't gonna listen. Her and Dawn are hardheaded."

"Don't let them work for you no more. They won't have a choice but to get a job. Them girls are materialistic like hell. They ain't trying to be broke," Monique said with concern filling her voice. She knew firsthand how the streets would eat you alive and spit you out. She barely made it out of the very same streets Mecca and Dawn were now on, and she wanted better for them.

"All they'll do is go to work for someone else, and they won't treat them like I do. Or they'll become strippers or hookers or something, and I'm not trying to hear that, Mo," Ruby said in a matter-of-fact tone. Monique knew when to back off. The last thing a person wanted to do was piss Ruby off. She was liable to do anything with no remorse.

Ruby rented Mecca and Dawn an apartment in Sutter Gardens, an apartment complex in the East New York section of Brooklyn. The neighborhood was just as dangerous as Mecca's Brownsville environment, but she would have it no other way. Her reason for staying in the slums was simple.

"If niggas think you hiding, they'll come looking. If you in their face, they know you ready for whatever."

Ruby also bought Mecca and Dawn Volkswagen Jettas. Mecca's was china blue, Dawns was silver.

Mecca and Dawn pulled up in their Jettas at a basketball tournament in Miller Park in East

New York. Even though there were hustlers out there with Benzes and BMWs, Sterlings, and Alfa Romeo Milanos, the two young chicks made everyone look in their direction.

They wore black body suits that hugged the curves on their well-developed frames. Mecca wore a pair of red snakeskin boots and Dawn had black lizard-skin boots. They both wore large bracelets that resembled Wonder Woman's and giant doorknocker earrings. They both kept their hair laced with Anita Baker hairdos.

As Mecca and Dawn exited their vehicles, two cars pulled up behind them. One of the luxury cars blasted Big Daddy Kane's "Ain't No Halfed Steppin'" and the other blasted KRS One's "My Philosophy." They were a vintage, candy-apple red 1950 Jaguar XK and a sky blue Porsche.

The young cats that emerged from the vehicles were all decked out in the latest gear and jewelry. The driver of the Porsche stood out the most with his Gucci short set and sneakers. His diamond-flooded Figueroa chain with Mary holding baby Jesus was the size of Slick Rick's chain. He had a high rise pinky ring flooded with ice as well. He and Mecca caught each other's eyes and he smiled at her. Mecca looked away. At sixteen years of age, Mecca was still a virgin, unlike many of her peer group. Mecca was more into making money and fashion than boys. Also Mecca was afraid to fall for a boy after seeing how it had affected her aunt when Wise broke her heart.

Besides all that, Mecca had to stay focused. It took a lot for her to prove to Ruby that she could handle the responsibility that was given to her. When it came to business, Ruby didn't take any shorts, and since she was able to convince Ruby that helping her out was a better choice than going back to school, she had no choice but to stay on top of her game.

"It's not good to fall in love with no nigga because all they do is use you for sex. That's all they want, they care nothing about your feelings. So to avoid being hurt, don't fall in love. Use them for what you need the same way they do us," Ruby had always reminded Mecca.

During the game, the guy in the Gucci short set stared at Mecca. She glanced at him as she walked around the park with Dawn. Other girls in the park glared at her and Dawn with envy. All the boys in the park were either staring at the duo or trying to get with them. Dawn flirted with some, then she stopped and talked to one of the members of the guy who wore the Gucci short set's crew. She found out that crew was from Brownsville Houses and Dawn thought one of the guys looked familiar, but she couldn't place his face right away. She figured if they didn't know Mecca or Mecca didn't know them, then most likely it was the stick up crew that was sticking up Ruby's spot in the projects. Her suspicions were confirmed when the guy with the Gucci suit walked up to the guy she spoke to.

"Son, tell shorty to tell her friend I'm trying to get with her. Shorty look right," the guy in Gucci said.

"Yo, Dawn, tell ya girl my man Tah wanna talk to her!"

Dawn took another good look at him and remembered his face from when they were in junior high. Her mind flashed back to the girl Tamika, who she and Mecca jumped and Mecca cut her face because she thought Mecca was messing with her boyfriend Tah. Tah had dropped out of school, and since Dawn and Mecca never went back to school after that, Mecca never got the chance to see what he looked like. Dawn thought better than to ask him about Tamika or explain why she asked. One of the guys in his crew could be related to Tamika and might want to get some payback for the lifetime scar Tamika wore on her face.

"Son, they from the ville," Tah's friend said to him about Mecca and Dawn.

"Word?" Tah asked, pointing at Dawn. "I knew you looked familiar. Where you live at in the ville?" he asked. Dawn just flashed him a flirtatious smile and sauntered over to where Mecca was sitting.

Mecca sat on the bleachers, drinking a wine cooler, watching the two teams, one in white uniforms with Brownsville written in black letters on the jersey and the other in purple uniforms that had East New York in white letters on the jersey, running a full court.

"Girl, you won't guess who the nigga in the Gucci short set is!" Dawn said, sitting next to Mecca.

Mecca swallowed the drink and, still watching the game, responded, "Who is he?"

"Remember that chick Tamika? We beat her ass in school and you cut her?" Dawn asked as Mecca looked at her attentively. "That's the boy she thought you were messing with," Dawn answered.

Mecca looked over at Tah, and she found him to be attractive. He was a caramel-complexioned, brown-eyed brother who stood about six feet tall. He had a medium build, not too big and not too small. He wore a fade-style haircut. The top of his hair was wavy with the sides faded. Mecca laughed at the thought of Tamika approaching her about a boy Mecca never met.

"They from Brownsville Houses. You never seen them?" Dawn asked.

Mecca shook her head, looking at the crew to see if she recognized any of them. Mecca didn't. "Nah, I don't know them."

"Well, the boy in the Gucci short set wanna meet you. He said you a cutie," Dawn said.

She didn't want to tell Mecca the guy's name because she thought maybe it wasn't the stick up crew. If it was, if Mecca got with him he would stop, and Mecca wouldn't have to worry about the crew anymore because she would be dating the leader. Plus, she needed to get her cherry popped. Tah came and sat next to Mecca on the bleachers while his friend grabbed Dawn's hand and led her off the bleachers to talk privately.

"What's your name, shorty?" Tah, asked showing his bottom teeth that were covered with gold.

"Mecca," she said tersely.

Tah nodded his head. "That's a pretty name. It fits."

Mecca smiled and thought *he can't come up with something more original?* How many times had she heard that? She turned to look at him.

"You nervous or something?" she asked.

"Me?" Tah asked, pointing to his chest with a confused look on his face. "Hell no, why should I be nervous?" Tah asked, shaking his head.

"'Cause I know you can come up with something more original instead of my name is pretty, it fits!"

"You buggin'. I really meant it!" Tah said, sounding sincere. "I don't need to borrow lines from no one, shorty. I call it like I see it." Mecca ignored him and continued to watch the game.

"So what's your name? What do they call you?" she asked.

"Tah."

"Oh, yeah, Tah. You're Tamika's boyfriend!" Mecca said.

Tah snapped his head back, surprised to hear his ex's name spoken from a total stranger. He gave her a look like he was trying to remember her from somewhere else or place her face from someone he may have met in the past.

"That's old news, shorty. How you know though?"

Mecca giggled. "I used to go to school with her and she thought I was messing with you, because I guess you looked at me one day when you picked her up from school."

"I knew you looked familiar!" Tah said. "Oh shit! You ain't the one who blast Mika on her face?" Tah asked, making a mock slashing with his hand. He remembered seeing Mecca in passing at school, but never saw her after the fight she had with his then girlfriend.

"She shouldn't have come up on me like that," Mecca replied with candor.

"Okay, shorty. You a wild one on the hush," Tah said.

"I told you my name. Stop calling me shorty!" Mecca barked.

When she thought of his name again, it hit her. One of Ruby's workers in Brownsville Houses said a crew led by a nigga named Tah was sticking them up. Mecca didn't want to bring it up yet. If it was him, she didn't want to wake him up to who she was. She had to investigate first. If it was him, she would have to formulate a plot on how to stop him. *Then*, Mecca thought, *getting to know him could be part of my investigation of Tah and his crew.*

"I'm sorry, Mecca. Calling you shorty is just a figure of speech. I'm not trying to be disrespectful at all," Tah replied before asking, "Do you have a man?"

"No, I don't," Mecca replied.

"I hear you from Langston Hughes. That's up the block from Brownsville. Maybe I can give you a call or come take you out one night. You know, a movie and a bite to eat," Tah said.

The way her attitude was, Tah thought she would deny giving him the number and say she would see him around, letting him down easy.

To his surprise, Mecca said she would give him her number for him to call later. Tah smiled, then reached in his back pocket and pulled out a pen. He reached in his front pocket, and pulled out a hundred-dollar bill to write the number on. Mecca thought he was fronting. She grabbed the money and wrote her number on it. She stood up, ready to leave the bleachers to find Dawn, and she gave Tah a seductive look.

"Hopefully, I'll hear from you soon."

Tah put the money in his pocket. "Oh, you will," he replied, looking back at her and letting his eyes undress her.

When Mecca met Dawn, she grabbed Dawn's hand, pulling her away from Tah's friend. "Call me!" Dawn yelled to the boy as Mecca pulled.

"Dawn, I think these are the niggas robbing my aunt's spot in Brownsville Houses!"

"Word?" Dawn responded as if she was shocked at the thought that she already had.

"Yeah, remember I told you the worker said some nigga name Tah and his peoples were robbing them?"

"Yeah."

"I'm not sure, but I'm almost sure it's them. I'm going to find out. I'ma hang out with that nigga, Tah," Mecca said before the girls entered their own cars.

Dawn shook her head and thought, *Mecca is as crazy as her aunt, and if it is Tah and his crew robbing Ruby's spots, and if Tah doesn't catch on to what Mecca is up to, he'll be dead within a few weeks.*

Two days had passed since Mecca had given Tah her phone number. On the third day he called, and he and Mecca spoke for hours. They talked about the people they both knew in Brownsville. Mecca joked about Tah and Tamika's relationship.

"What you did to her? She must have been really in love with you."

They both laughed when Tah responded."I don't know. There's something about me I can't figure out. Maybe it's my chain?"

Mecca found talking to Tah easy to do. He was smart and funny. He made her laugh the entire conversation. Mecca found herself unintentionally opening up to him. She began telling him things that she planned on not telling him. Mecca told him that she lived in Sutter Gardens on Blake and Hendrix Street, and she told him she was a virgin, which excited Tah and made him want her even more.

On their first date, Tah took Mecca to a Tony Roma's restaurant in Queens. Riding in Tah's Porsche made Mecca want one. She reminded herself to save up money to get one. Mecca was surprised at how much of a gentleman he was. He opened doors for her and he picked her up with roses in his hands. Tah took her to Coney Island where they walked on the beach. They took pictures together holding each other. He never let Mecca pay for anything, even when she begged him to let her pay for at least a movie.

"It would make me feel less than a man if I let a woman pay for anything," Tah would tell her.

Mecca realized Tah was a man of pride. Mecca got so caught up with Tah that she forgot why she started seeing him in the first place. Just like Dawn predicted, when Tah and Mecca got together, the workers in Brownsville Houses didn't have any problems with Tah and his crew. What Mecca and Dawn didn't know was that Tah was extorting Stone. Stone paid a thousand dollars a week for them not to rob the spot. Stone paid him out of his own pay.

When Tah wasn't around, Mecca found herself missing him. All she talked about to Dawn was Tah. Dawn was happy for her. She noticed Mecca's attitude change since she had started seeing Tah. Her explosive temper simmered down. Mecca usually was not someone who smiled, but she had a smile on her face almost all the time. Ruby noticed the change in her niece and she expressed it to Monique to see if

Monique could shed some light on why Mecca's attitude changed.

"What's up with Mecca? She's been acting different lately," Ruby said.

"You acted the same way when you were in love," Monique replied.

"Love!" Ruby yelled, not believing the words that came out of Monique's mouth. "She's in love with who?" she asked, sounding angered by the news.

"Some guy in the ville."

"Why she ain't tell me?" Ruby asked, this time sounding hurt. She thought she and Mecca had the kind of relationship where they could talk about these kinds of things.

"Because she knew you would act the way you acting now. You got to let her be, Ruby. You said it before: she knows how to handle herself."

"I just thought she would share something like that with me. At least let me see the cat, you know." Ruby sighed. When Mecca finally got around to telling Ruby, she didn't react the way Mecca expected, and it shocked Mecca.

"Don't rush to give up the pussy, Mecca. Make him wait until he proves he deserves it."

Mecca said she would take Ruby's advice. She told Ruby things that Tah did for her, and she showed her the diamond tennis bracelet he bought for her. It was Monique that Mecca confided in most about her relationship with Tah, and it made Ruby jealous. Monique was happy for Mecca but warned her about how guys could be.

"It's risky dealing with niggas who are in the streets. You got to be prepared for him going to jail or getting killed. It's gonna hurt real bad, Mecca, so be careful with your heart."

"I hear you, but I love this nigga, Mo," Mecca revealed, feeling like she was already in too deep.

Chapter Eight

Y'all some "well wishers," friendly acting, envy hiding snakes . . .

Nas

"This is crumbs compared to what you could get from her," Stone complained to Tah while he handed him the $1,000 he gave him a week not to rob Ruby's houses. Both men stood in the pissy-smelling dark hallway of a building in Brownsville.

"You talking about that bitch with the green Sterling? You work for a bitch?" Tah asked, grinning and shaking his head. "Damn, Stone, you really fell off. How the fuck you let it get to that point?"

"It ain't as sweet as you think it is, Tah. She ain't your average bitch, kid. That bitch is a stone cold murderer. Remember Darnell from Langston Hughes? It was her that threw that nigga out the window. I don't think you knew Wise, but she bodied that nigga, too. She's the real deal, Tah," Stone warned, holding his head down, ashamed. Tah, with menace and anger in his tone, put his finger in Stone's face and gave him a warning as well.

"Nigga, I'm the real deal. Ain't no bitch or nobody else going to put fear in my heart. You's a bitch-ass, washed-up nigga. I ain't like you, mu'fucka. You just get that bitch to bring something heavy to you. Tell her somebody you know want three of them pies, and I'll take it from there."

Stone nodded grimly, agreeing to the setup. The pressure that Tah put on Stone, coupled with the fear of Ruby possibly finding out that Stone agreed to help set her up, caused Stone to relapse, and he started smoking crack again. When he got paid, the monkey on his back caused him to even cop crack from the workers he collected money from for Ruby. To his demise, word got back to Ruby that he was smoking again. When she confronted him about it he denied it, and she was full of anger.

"This nigga tryna insult my intelligence, Mo," Ruby said to Monique back at her Hamptons villa.

"Bitch, you must really be pissed. I'm down here with all your pussy in my face, and you rambling on about Stone," Monique complained to Ruby from her place in between Ruby's thighs while Ruby sat in a beach chair out on the patio.

Monique wiped Ruby's wetness from her face with a pink beach towel, opened up the sliding glass door and marched into the house, angry and naked. Ruby took a puff on her blunt, and blew circles into the air before she yelled for Monique to come back.

"Mo, come here. I'm sorry."

Ten minutes later, Monique appeared on the patio fully dressed in a sexy, tight-fitting pair of Gap jeans, a white button-down shirt from the Gap as well, with a cute pair of Gucci stiletto sandals to match the Gucci hobo bag dangling from her wrist.

"You need me to bring something back? I'm driving to the city," Monique asked Ruby, not bothering to make eye contact.

"I'm sorry, Mo. I'm just stressed a little, you know?" Ruby replied, pleading for forgiveness with her eyes.

"Yeah, I know. Do you need anything?" Monique asked again, not willing to forgive Ruby that easily.

"When you coming back?" Ruby asked her, now seeing her through a weed-filled daze. Monique just shook her head.

"I'll be back by midnight."

"Bring me back some cheesecake from Juniors."

Monique drove Ruby's Sterling into the city. She knew in order to get Ruby's attention back on their love life she'd have to get rid of whatever it was that got in the way. What got in the way was Stone. Monique felt for the nickel-plated .45 in her Gucci bag as she drove the two-hour drive into Brooklyn. While driving, she half listened to the New Edition tape that was playing. She loved the sound of Johnny Gill's voice when he sang "Can You Stand The Rain."

When Monique reached the dark, grimy streets of Brownsville, she drove to Rockaway and Dumont where Stone usually hung out. There were groups of hustlers and stick up kids standing on the corners. Some waved to Monique and some just stared at the Sterling as it drove by. Everyone knew Ruby drove the Sterling, but the mirror-tinted windows blocked anyone from seeing Monique driving it. She looked in front of a brightly lit liquor store and in front of a few bodegas and couldn't find Stone.

Monique then drove to the block she hated going to: Mother Gaston Boulevard and Sutter Avenue. Stone usually hung out up there, either at the gas station or on the opposite corner. He wasn't there, either. Driving around her birthplace, her native Brownsville, Monique looked at the neighborhood like an outsider. She could not believe the decaying, dilapidated houses were occupied by human beings. Living in the Hamptons made her beloved Brownsville leave a bad taste in her mouth.

She could not believe she felt this way. What was wrong with her? This is where she was from. This place made her who she was, and she loved who she was. She inhaled deeply in thought. *I love the ville. If it ain't rough it ain't right.*

Monique drove to what was said to be the most dangerous projects in the ville, Brownsville Houses. She drove around the projects looking for Stone, but still didn't see him. She noticed groups of young men sitting on benches with boom boxes blasting the latest hip-hop joints. The neighborhood was noisy with music and hustlers yelling, "I got those red tops over here!" You could hear mothers yelling to their kids to come in the house. Groups of extension-wearing young girls with big, gold earrings and bangles walked around the projects, flirting with much older men. Some were looking for their baby fathers for money or trying to catch them messing with some other girl.

Monique smiled at what used to be her way of living. She felt a sense of pride now. Places like Brownsville make a person appreciate the little things in life. People who live in the Hamptons and other suburban getaways don't know what it's like to be dirt poor, and would kill themselves if they ever had to go through it. People in Brownsville are survivors. That's what Monique was, a survivor.

Monique stopped at a light on Rockaway Avenue in Brownsville Houses waiting for it to turn green. She looked at a group of men in front of one of the tan and brown buildings to see if she spotted Stone among them. With her focus on the men in front of the building, she never got the chance to see the teenager dressed all in black walk up to the passenger-side window with his .44 Magnum pointed at the tinted glass. The loud shots from the gun could be heard within a five-block radius.

Monique heard the first shot clearly. The rest were muffled and her vision became blurry. Everything began to turn dark, and her hearing faded out. She didn't hear the teenager yell, "That's for Darnell, bitch!" People in the projects saw the teen run from the car while the horn blared from the weight of Monique's slumped body pressing against the wheel. Stone heard the gunshots while he loaded his stem with crack while sitting on the staircase on the roof of a Brownsville Houses building. One of Ruby's workers ran up the stairs while Stone inhaled the lit crack inside.

"Yo, Stone! Somebody just bodied that chick Ruby. She's slumped in her Sterling on Rockaway right now!"

Stone almost choked on the smoke he inhaled when he heard what the worker said. He had to see it with his own eyes. He couldn't believe Ruby slipped up and got herself killed. He started thinking Ruby was invincible, that she couldn't be touched. He knew how cautious she was. She trusted no one except Mecca. Stone didn't even think she trusted her lover Monique.

Stone ran down the stairs thinking it couldn't be Ruby. *Nah, not Ruby!* He ran toward Rockaway Avenue still not believing what he just heard. When he saw the Sterling he still couldn't believe it. He saw a crackhead he knew reaching inside of the car with the driver-side door open.

"Yo, Smoke, get the fuck away from her!" Stone yelled as he approached the car. The smoker backed up out of the car, holding a gold chain in his hand.

"She won't be needing this, Stone. She deader than a mu'fucka, man."

"Smoke, put that shit down before I peel your skull back, nigga," Stone said, pointing a .38 revolver at him. The crackhead dropped the gold chain and ran off, not wanting to test Stone's patience. Stone approached the car, putting his gun back on his waist. He exhaled loudly when he realized it wasn't Ruby.

"Damn, Monique. What the fuck you doing over here, girl?"

Stone heard police and ambulance sirens headed toward the scene and he didn't want to get caught up out there. He walked over to the pay phone a few blocks down and paged Ruby.

The backdrop of Mecca's vision of a white-robed man named Lou changed from bright light to total darkness. Lou's robe turned blood red. Mecca looked at herself for the first time, noticing she was naked. Seeing Monique killed made her cry. She wasn't there when it happened, but seeing exactly how it went down hurt her to her soul.

"I don't want to do this anymore. Why are you doing this?" she sobbed.

"Monique loved you, Mecca. She didn't want you in the streets. Not only did she express that to your aunt, but she also told you plenty of times to get it together. You didn't listen. Or was it that you didn't take her seriously because she continued to play the game?" Lou asked.

Mecca still shook her head, sobbing. "I don't know! I don't know!" Mecca sobbed as she heard Monique's voice in her ears warning her about the streets:

"Mecca, don't be like me and your aunt. You see what happened to your moms and pops. Your mom wasn't even in the game like that, but she still died for what your pop was into. You got your whole life ahead of you. You don't want to die young, or end up in jail forever. These streets don't discriminate. Just because you're a pretty girl don't mean shit. You can't change the direction of a bullet with a fat ass and good looks."

"And you know what, Mecca?" Lou continued, "She wasn't the only one who wanted what was best for you. You were blinded by greed and lust."

Lou posed with his hands on his waist like a female posing for a photo shoot and said, "You were a diva in the streets. You were invincible, right, Mecca? Nobody could touch the Queen of

New York." Lou laughed out loud, then, just as quickly, his expression turned serious.

"You were wrong though, but it's my job to show you what you failed to see. Let's carry on," he said, clapping his palms together to continue Mecca's journey.

Chapter Nine

For she hath cast down many wounded; yea, many strong men have been slain by her.
Psalms 7:26

Hundreds of people convened in the Brownsville funeral home to pay their respects to Monique. Monique's oak wood casket was surrounded by expensive wreaths and flowers paid for by Ruby and Mecca. Ruby paid for the funeral, the casket, and the mausoleum that Monique's body would be laid in to rest.

Ruby had Monique's body dressed in a white pants suit with gold buttons down the front of the jacket. She made sure Monique was made up beautifully. She almost looked more elaborately dressed and made up as a corpse than she did alive. Some people commented on that fact out of earshot. When people tried to hug Ruby, offering her their condolences, people she didn't know or had ever seen Monique associate with, she verbally assaulted them.

"Who are you? Did you even know Monique?" To some of Monique's family members, she growled as they walked by.

"Stop being phony, when was the last time y'all saw her? What you do, chew an onion to get them fake-ass tears in your eyes?" she asked as they came up to view the body, causing everyone to avoid her.

She paid her workers to keep their eyes open. If they find out who killed Monique, she wanted to know. She offered a $50,000 hit for the person who found the person. She had a plan for Stone's ass too, who showed up at the wake high off crack, and smelling like he hadn't bathed in months. He went up to view Monique's body, and Ruby gave him a look that he missed. He was definitely going to pay.

"Ruby, I'm gonna find out who did this. I swear to God, someone is gonna pay!" Stone whispered in her ear before he walked away. Little did he know he would have to pay for this too.

Damn near every killer in Brownsville tried to cash in on the hit. There were thousands of rumors about who did it. When the rumor of Tah's involvement spread around the streets, Mecca quickly put an end to that, letting everyone know that Tah was with her that night.

It was the most memorable night in Mecca's life. After she and Tah dined at Red Lobster, Tah rented a room at the Ramada Inn near LaGuardia Airport. Mecca sat in the passenger seat of Tah's Porsche feeling the wind blow against her face as Tah sped down the Van Wyck Expressway. She tried to mentally prepare herself for the physical act of sex. She had never been this nervous, except when she first felt the flow of blood leak from her vagina. Instead of running to talk to Ruby about her period, she confided in Monique.

"Monique, come here," Mecca whispered from the bathroom, standing behind the door and sticking her head out.

"What's up, girl?" Monique asked, concerned.

Mecca opened the door all the way and pulled Monique into the bathroom by her hand. She showed her the drops of blood on the panties she held in her hand, and Monique started laughing. Mecca was confused.

"Why you laughing, Mo? I'm bleeding!"

"Girl, ain't no reason for you to be scared. It's your period. It's all a part of being a woman. It's going to happen every month, so get used to it," Monique said, opening the door. "Stay right here, I'll be right back." When Monique returned, she handed Mecca a Maxi pad.

"Put this on your pussy, and change it throughout the day until you stop bleeding. It usually takes three to seven days. Here is a bag of pads. I'll get you a douche to clean yourself afterward. You don't want your pussy smelling like trash truck juice."

Mecca sat at the funeral home staring at Monique's body, thinking of her. She felt a lump in her throat as she tried not to cry. Monique wouldn't be here to talk to her about sex, and she didn't think sex was a topic Ruby wanted to speak to her about. Mecca's mind wandered back to that night with Tah, and it saddened her how she wouldn't have anyone to talk to now. That was one of the most memorable nights of her life, and she zoned out as she thought back.

"You all right?" Tah asked, seeing Mecca's facial expression in deep thought. "If you're not with it we can wait, Mecca."

"No, I'm all right. I don't want to wait any longer. I love you, Tah." Mecca sucked her teeth before responding to him.

Tah was caught off guard with the four-letter word that he swore he would never say or feel toward a woman except his mother or grandmother. Too many cats he knew fell victim to that word. He knew dudes who fell in love with a chick, got locked up, and the girl the dude loved was in the free world fucking the dude's friends, brothers, and even the nigga's sister.

A lot of cats got killed over women, and Tah swore to himself that it would never be him. He really liked Mecca a lot, though. He even dared to say he cared about her. She wasn't like the girls he usually dealt with. She wasn't the neighborhood freak like the girls he and his crew got a piece of. She was a virgin, and she wanted him to be her first. That sent Tah on an ego trip so far he had to pack a year's worth of luggage. But love? That's a whole other level that Tah didn't think he was ready for. Not wanting to ruin the night, Tah told Mecca he loved her too, and was almost convinced that he believed it.

Tah and Mecca entered the plush hotel room with cream wall-to-wall carpeting, mirrored walls, and a Jacuzzi shaped like a martini glass. Tah surprised her with a pair of hoop earrings with diamonds on them. Mecca hugged Tah, then their mouths met and their tongues began to wrestle with each other. Tah tried to be as gentle as he could. He wanted this night to be special for her. He wanted her to be strung out on him and never want to share her love with anyone else. He felt he was experienced enough to pull it off.

Tah began to suck on Mecca's earlobe, then slowly moved down to her neck. Mecca felt chills through her whole body as Tah began to unbutton her shirt. Her black satin bra came into view, and Tah had to make himself slow down. He picked her up and walked her over to the king-sized bed to lay her down, afterward softly kissing her belly button while caressing her breast. Then suddenly he stopped.

"Hold on, Mecca. Let me use the bathroom."

Tah went into the bathroom and looked at himself in the large mirror over the beige porcelain sink. His manhood bulged against the crotch of his red Fila velour sweat suit. As was routine with every girl he bedded, Tah took out his dick and began to masturbate so that when he had sex with Mecca he wouldn't cum quick. Mecca unhooked her bra while she waited for Tah to take off her tight-fitting jeans. Her panties matched her bra. Remembering what Monique had said about keeping her pussy smelling fresh, Mecca rubbed her hand against her pussy and smelled it. She was satisfied with the smell the vinegar-and-water douche left behind.

She heard plenty of tales from being around guys in the projects and listening to the workers she collected money from of a girl's pussy smelling like fish chasing a nigga away. The news that a girl had a stink pussy spread around the neighborhood and did severe damage to a girl's reputation. Mecca made sure that it would never be her. Three minutes later, Tah came out of the bathroom ready to give Mecca the best first sexual experience ever.

Tah took off his pants and crawled on the bed in his Calvin Klein boxers. He looked at Mecca's body and he felt his dick begin to stiffen. Her firm breasts and plump rear end didn't fit a sixteen-year-old's body. Her body fit a woman in her twenties. Mecca could tell that Tah worked out. He wasn't bulky or too small; his body was well defined from the eighteen-month sentence he served in D.F.Y.

Tah let his tongue explore Mecca's body, taking her on a high she had never experienced before. She gasped when she felt his warm tongue on her nipples. He licked down her belly button while removing her jeans and panties. He continued to taste and caress Mecca until he was sure she liked what he was doing.

"Tah, that feels so good," she moaned.

Mecca tried to get away from Tah, but it felt too good. She felt waves of pleasure run through her body. She didn't know why she kept feeling her entire body when Tah put his tongue inside of her. He brought her to multiple orgasms in no time.

He wanted to loosen her up some; the tightness of her pussy made Tah grind his teeth. Not that Mecca was his first virgin, but she felt a lot tighter than previous ones he had encountered. Slowly he opened her legs in the missionary position, and glided his rock-hard dick inside of her.

"Wait . . . wait, Tah. It hurts!" Mecca screamed out loud, holding on to Tah tightly. Tah kissed Mecca's lips and whispered in her ear to calm her down.

"I'm sorry, Mecca. I didn't mean to hurt you."

"I know, Tah. Please try again, I want you in me."

After Tah's first orgasm, he took Mecca into the Jacuzzi and they enjoyed a bottle of Moët while they relaxed. Tah stared at Mecca and it reminded him of something his partner Boogie had told him awhile back, and it had him feeling confused.

"Yo, Tah. Your chick Mecca is the bitch with the Sterling niece."

"Get the fuck outta here, Boog!" Tah responded in disbelief.

"Word is born, son. Your chick work for her aunt, too. She manages her spots in the projects."

"How you know all this, son?" Tah asked, not wanting to believe what he was hearing.

"You heard of Blast right?" Boog asked, and Tah nodded his head, indicating that he remembered. "That's her pops. Darnell bodied her mom and pop and her aunt took her in. That bitch from Langston Hughes."

"Mecca, let me ask you something," Tah said as he took a sip from his glass of Moët.

"Go ahead, ask me whatever," she answered, hoping he wasn't going to back out on her.

"Where you be getting money from? How you get all that fly gear?" Tah asked, registering the look on her face. The smile left Mecca's face. His question surprised her. She wondered why he asked that after all this time they been together. Mecca put her head down, looking at the bubbling water.

"My parents are dead, and I get SSI checks."

It was true, Mecca did receive SSI, but it was a mere $500 a month. She put that in a bank account and spent the money she made working for her aunt on the things she had. Tah was glad that she didn't lie, figuring since he had heard her parents were dead, that just maybe she was getting SSI. He chalked up the idea that she may be working for her aunt as just a rumor.

"Damn, sorry to hear that. Do you mind me asking how they died?" Tah replied consolingly, hoping she would open up more to him.

"Yes, I do mind, so don't ask," Mecca said, cutting him off.

Tah watched Mecca's facial expression change into one that he had never seen on her before: the look of pure rage. It was more than rage; it was more like pure evil. Tah knew it was time to change the topic before the mood got messed up. Besides, he wanted some more pussy because his dick was hard again.

"I didn't mean to make you angry, Mecca. I'm sorry." Tah smiled, then reached over to kiss her.

He kissed her cheek, and his mouth traveled down her neck. He placed his hand between her thighs and his fingers found their way to her clit. The evil look on Mecca's face disappeared, and she expressed pure pleasure. Deciding to not even leave the Jacuzzi, Tah sexed Mecca in every position imaginable until the wee hours of the morning.

A week after Monique's death, Stone had just finished making his rounds at each of Ruby's spots. He stopped in Langston Hughes to chat with some of the workers who were mostly young teenagers whose parents were customers. Stone saw one of the workers running through the projects, and stopped to see what was happening.

By the time he and the other workers realized what the young guy was running from, they were all surrounded by unmarked cars, undercover detectives, and federal agents.

People in their apartments, and hoes standing outside in the area, heard cars screeching and the sound of police yelling for them to get on the ground and put their hands in the air before they blew their brains out. At the same time there were raids conducted in Langston Hughes, Ruby's spots in Brownsville and Coney Island were being raided as well. Ruby was watching an episode of *As The World Turns* when she heard a knock on the door. Dressed in only a long blue and yellow Polo robe with thong to match, she hated to have to get up from in front of the television, but she had no choice. She got off the couch and walked to the large, white double doors, grabbing hold of the gold-plated doorknobs.

"Who is it?" Ruby yelled on her way to the door.

"It's the police and we have a warrant. Open up!" an officer yelled through the door.

"Hold on, let me get dressed," Ruby yelled back, not knowing what move to make next.

"Open up, now!" the officer yelled before busting through the door and rushing Ruby to the floor before she had a chance to get one of her guns from the closet. Ruby didn't plan on getting arrested. She planned to go out in a gunfight, but it was too late.

"You have the right to remain silent. Anything you say can and will be used against you in a court of law. You have the right to an attorney . . ."

Chapter Ten

A faithful witness will not lie, but a false witness will utter lies.
Proverbs 14:4

The government had received information from a confidential informant about Ruby and her organization. The informant couldn't provide how much money Ruby was pulling in from her distribution of crack cocaine, but the government estimated that her gross amount was in the hundreds of thousands. So when the judge in the federal courthouse in Brooklyn placed Ruby's bail at $2 million, Ruby got out within a week.

The F.B.I. knew they stumbled onto an organization that was beyond your average drug gang. The informant either didn't know the part Mecca played in the organization or just didn't want her in jail. Stone's bail was set at $100,000, and Ruby made sure he was bailed out.

"What makes you think it's Stone?" Mecca asked innocently, not wanting to jump the gun.

"Who else could it be? Who else knows all about me besides you and him? Monique is gone!" Ruby yelled at Mecca as they sat in Mecca's Sutter Gardens apartment's living room.

Mecca's apartment was simply decorated. Her living room had a black, big pillowed couch, a forty-two-inch television that sat on a crystal television stand, and a six-disc Sony surround sound system that was surrounded by black art on the walls with cream frames to match the curtains she had hung at the window. Over the television she had a large picture of her parents that was hand drawn by a street artist, and a wooden wall unit with family pictures on it as well.

"He's a crackhead, Mecca. They'll do anything to get a hit. Those crackers probably gave him a hit just to snitch," Ruby said while trying to calm down.

"Why didn't he say anything to me or Dawn?" Mecca wondered out loud.

"Where is that bitch anyway?" Ruby asked skeptically.

"With her boyfriend," Mecca responded, but she had a skeptical look on her face. She didn't think Dawn would do anything like that. What would she gain from it?

All Dawn thinks about is that no-good boyfriend of hers. One of Tah's flunkies. Dawn hasn't been around lately since she met him, and that nigga has her strung out. Then Mecca remembered something that Dawn said, and it made her wonder:

"Mecca, I think we better leave this game alone. I feel like something bad is gonna happen if we keep going on like this. We gonna end up either in jail or dead."

"Don't go getting paranoid now, bitch. I can't just bounce up out the game like that," Mecca said to Dawn, not believing her ears. If it weren't for the game, they wouldn't have all the shit they had.

She brushed off the thought, concluding that Dawn was just paranoid at the time. Shit, she was the one who said they should get in the game in the first place.

"Since y'all bitches got them boyfriends y'all been on some real slackin' shit. Y'all let them niggas get the best of y'all. Mecca, you know better," Ruby scolded her, trying to talk some sense into Mecca to keep from punching her in her damn mouth.

"So what we gonna do?" Mecca asked, wanting to get off the boyfriend subject.

Ruby rubbed her temples and sighed. "I took a big loss. That bail really fucked me up. I got to get consignment off these Dominican mu'fuckas and start from scratch. What's up with these Sutter Garden niggas? They gettin' money?"

"Please. Those sorry-ass niggas hustle for outfits. You see the ones in front of the building? They stand there all day every day like they doing security and none of them niggas even got a Honda scooter. They some bus' ass niggas," Mecca replied, sucking her teeth.

"Those the types of mu'fuckas we want. Niggas who don't want much. That's how we get rich. If all they want is outfits then they will go hard for them. If we offer them more than what they got now, they'll gladly work for us. C'mon, Mecca, wake up, girl!" Ruby said, smiling.

Ruby kept quiet while she and Stone drove, then she parked on a small block on Twenty-third Street and Surface. The beach was at the end of the block. The block was deserted on the chilly night. Stone was always nervous in the presence of Ruby: he knew she was unpredictable and would kill in a heartbeat.

"Somebody snitching on us, Rube. We got to find out who did this. If you want, I'll handle this kid who got Mo—"

Ruby drew the .45 with a silencer so quick, Stone didn't have time to finish the sentence. His head exploded against the passenger side window as Ruby sent one bullet into his temple. Ruby got out of the driver's side and walked over to the passenger side. She opened the door and let Stone's body fall onto the sidewalk. She smiled when she heard the waves crashing into the beach. No one would hear her.

She went to the trunk of the car and removed a bottle of bleach and a dirty rag. She poured the bleach on the rag, stepped over Stone's body and wiped the blood off the window and door.

She looked at Stone's body and ripped open his black silk shirt to see if he was wired. He wasn't. She removed the gold Gucci link chain from his neck, and searched his black corduroy pants pocket, and removed $500 from his pocket. She left them turned inside out to make it look like he had been shot right there in the street. Ruby pumped more bullets in his head and body, and then she got back in the car and slowly drove off.

The next morning, Ruby drove into Manhattan with her hair in a ponytail, wearing a beige cotton skirt that reached her knees, a white blouse under a beige blazer, black sheer pantyhose to match, and black, five-inch heel shoes. The office of Gilmore, Stein and Bloomberg was located on Thirty-ninth Street and Park Avenue. Ruby walked in the office of Stanley Gilmore, Esq., the senior partner of the law firm. She had had him on retainer since 1987. He had a perfect record of all wins, no losses. She had met him through Stone.

Stone killed a Jamaican cat in front of the entire Langston Hughes projects during an annual Langston Hughes day, the day the project celebrated when it was built. Every project in New York has a day like that, as if the residents are celebrating the fact that they live in poverty-stricken, low-income projects with conditions a fence away from being a prison.

No one from the projects gave information to the police. There was no need to. Stone killed the man in the view of a housing cop walking the beat. Gilmore had the cop on the stand for almost two hours and when he was done with him, the jury was ready to convict the cop for the murder.

Ruby placed a brown paper bag on Gilmore's desk while he sat in his large, black leather recliner with an expensive, three-piece black, pinstriped suit resembling a 1920's Mafioso. He tried to conceal his receding hairline by combing the little hair he had left on the top of his bald spot.

"That's fifteen. I'll have the rest for you next week," Ruby said, sitting in one of the smaller leather chairs in front of Gilmore's large wooden desk. Gilmore grabbed the paper bag, looked in, and then placed the brown paper bag in one of the drawers in the desk.

"So how are things looking?" Ruby asked, folding her leg over the other, watching Gilmore stare at her finely toned thighs. Gilmore stood up and paced behind his desk with his hand in his pockets.

"I'm still waiting on the government to turn over the discovery. From what I do know," Gilmore said, pausing to face Ruby "there's an informant that gave up a lot of info. They're making it a RICO case. You getting out on that two million raised some flags in the IRS, too. How are you going to account for that?" he asked.

"My life savings and donations from friends to get me out," Ruby replied with a straight face.

Gilmore shook his head.

"I don't think that the government's going to buy that. What about the cars, the house in the Hamptons? They're gonna want to know how you went from a Brownsville housing project to the Hamptons with no job."

"You're my lawyer; tell me what should I do," Ruby barked.

Gilmore sighed. “As an officer of the court, I can’t give you incriminating advice.” Gilmore then smiled. “But as a friend, I can show you how to clean your cash.”

“You can’t find out who this snitch is now? I mean, pull some strings?” Ruby asked.

Gilmore walked to the front of his desk and sat on it in front of her. Ruby already figured she knew that Stone was the rat, but she wanted to make sure. She laughed inwardly about how she was able to convince Stone, who she knew was scared to death of her and probably knew she would figure he was a rat, to get in the car with her in the middle of the night and ride to Coney Island.

After bailing Stone out of the M.C.C. (Metropolitan Correctional Center) in Manhattan, she sent a message for Stone to meet her at the Stillwell Avenue train station in Coney Island. She wanted to discuss how they were going to get back in business. Knowing that Stone was smoking crack, when Stone got in the car, Ruby had a crack pipe in her hand, and before she drove off, she acted as if she needed to take a hit from the pipe. Stone stared at Ruby in disbelief.

Ruby sparked the lighter, held the fire at the end of the pipe, and inhaled the weed she had placed in the pipe. She opened the window and blew the smoke out of it. She looked at Stone and grinned.

"You know a bitch do this once in a blue. You wanna hit?" Ruby asked, reaching in her pocket and pulling out a small vial of crack.

She held out the stem to Stone. Stone snatched the vial out of her hand, and the stem, and with hands shaking he bit the top off the vial, removing the yellow top. He poured the pebble in the stem.

Ruby handed him the lighter. Stone inhaled the crack smoke deeply and held it in his lungs as long as possible. He spoke while holding his breath.

"Damn, Ruby, I ain't know you fuck around."

"Yeah, once in a while. A bitch be stressed, ya know." Ruby drove, looking at the road.

It was just that easy for Ruby to put him at ease so he wouldn't expect her to put bullets in him while they were both high off crack. Stone thought that if Ruby found out he was smoking crack she would kill him. To see her doing it made him feel comfortable around her, and that was his demise.

"It depends. I can definitely pull some strings, but I'm taking a big risk," Gilmore continued, still grinning at Ruby and staring at her well-built calves. Ruby stood up in front of Gilmore and grabbed him by the crotch.

"I know what you want, you freaky mu'fucka!" Grinning, she unzipped his pants and pulled out his small, shriveled-up, pinkish penis and gave him a hand job. While she jerked his dick, she smacked him on his face hard. He smiled.

"You like that, huh, you cracka!" Ruby growled, stroking him faster, thinking, *Men are so simple. The things they will do for a nut.* They are all the same. "If you cum in my hand, I'll beat the shit out of your old ass," Ruby threatened.

"I won't, just don't stop," Gilmore moaned, holding the corner of the desk tightly. He reached on his desk for a piece of tissue in a Kleenex box.

"Oh God! I'm cummin'. . . ."

Mecca felt someone placing a robe on her naked body. She couldn't see who it was. When she turned her head, it was dark. She looked down at her body, and a white linen robe was covering her. Lou stood with his arms folded, still in a red robe.

"How much death and mayhem does it take for a person to realize that what they are into is wrong?" Lou asked. He then counted on his fingers and said, "Your parents, Darnell, Wise, Monique, Stone. Then your aunt goes to jail and everybody involved in the organization except you and Dawn are caught up. You didn't see the blessing in that, huh?"

"Blessing! What blessing? Where's the blessing in death and jail?" Mecca yelled.

Lou became angry and it could be heard in his raised voice. "The fact that it didn't happen to you. That's the blessing!" He paused, then shook his head and continued in a low tone. "But, once again, Mecca, you had a veil over your eyes. It's all a game, right, Mecca?"

"Why you gotta yell like that? I can hear you," Mecca snapped, causing Lou to laugh.

"We all know you can hear. You just have a problem seeing. We all know you can hear, but you don't listen. Soon you're going to see and listen to what you didn't listen to before, whether you like it or not."

Chapter Eleven

Every wise woman buildeth her houses but foolish plucketh it down with her hands.

Proverbs 14

"I don't care who's first or who's last, I just know y'all better rock this at the drop of a dime, baby!" Marley Marl screamed on the intro of "The Symphony," a collaboration of Master Ace, Craig G, Kool G Rap, and Big Daddy Kane as Mecca and Dawn walked through the crowd on the dance floor of the Union Square club in Manhattan. This was a crowd Mecca and Dawn didn't stand out in, regardless that Mecca wore a Louis Vuitton three-quarter jacket with the matching boots, and bucket hat with the brim flipped up, while Dawn wore the same getup, but the brand name was Gucci.

There were people in the club from all five boroughs and surrounding areas like Mount Vernon, Yonkers, and Jersey who came to the Union Square in their best. There were girls and guys in full-length minks, shoes and boots from various reptiles, diamond- studded jewelry from neck to wrist, and mouths full of gold. Moët was the main beverage. The high rollers had cases of Dom Pérignon at their disposal.

It wasn't unusual to run into hip-hop celebrities in the crowd. Nice & Smooth, Doug E. Fresh, and Special Ed were in attendance. The crowd was usually split into groups according to the group's geographical location in the city. The Harlem cats stood in one corner, the Bronx cats in another, and the Queens cats had theirs. The Brooklyn cats usually were spread out, scheming on people to remove their jewelry or clothing from. Along with their fake IDs, Mecca and Dawn came with razor blades hidden under their collars, taped with Scotch tape. Before Mecca taped a razor to Dawn's collar, Dawn asked why they needed them.

"Just in case some jealous-ass bitch gets out of line, or some drunk nigga tries to touch you. You know how niggas is."

When Big Daddy Kane's "Ain't No Half Steppin'" roared through the club, the crowd reacted enthusiastically. Some wallflowers hit the dance floor, screaming, "That's my shit!" while other groups of cats who didn't dance leaned against the walls giving other cats evil stares.

If the crowd of guys made up of Harlemites didn't look in a certain direction, Mecca and Dawn would have never noticed Tah and his crew walk in the club, most of them wearing camouflage jackets with Champion hooded sweat shirts under the jacket, black jeans, and black Timberlands. Mecca noticed Tah didn't have any of his jewelry on, and he and his crew looked at the crowd as if they were looking at everyone individually for someone. Dawn was about to walk over to them, seeing her boyfriend with Tah, when Mecca grabbed her by her shoulder.

"Chill out, Dawn. Don't go over there. Them niggas look like they up to something, and it's something you don't wanna get caught in the middle of."

Dawn looked around the club and noticed girls and guys who were showcasing their jewelry moments ago stuff their chains inside their shirts. Some girls put their earrings in their pockets and some headed to the exit. To add to the fear and tension lingering in the air, the D.J., who was from Brooklyn, put on a Slick Rick song called "The Moment I Feared" where Slick Rick spits,

"Boogie Down was performin' hey they ain't no joke/ And a bunch of Brooklyn kids was lookin' all down my throat/ Was it my big chains with the big plates on 'em?/ Then they rolled on me and told me to run 'em/ This was the moment I feared."

Tah and his crew split up and walked around the club. Tah made his way to the bar and bought a bottle of Dom P. He grinned at some women at the bar, who probably thought that because of the way he looked he wouldn't be able to afford Dom Pérignon. They could tell he was from Brooklyn, and Brooklyn cats had a reputation of not being high rollers, but cats who lived off of robbery. Mecca stepped in front of him, rolling her eyes at the women at the bar.

"What's up, nigga? What you doing here?"

"The question is, what you doing here?" Tah shot back.

"I told you I was coming here tonight. Me and Dawn." Mecca smiled and grabbed Tah's hand. "Dance with me."

Tah pulled his hand away and smirked. "Dance! I look like the type of nigga to dance? You buggin', Mecca."

Mecca figured Tah wasn't the dancing type but she wanted to avoid him getting into trouble, and possibly getting hurt or going to jail. A lot of niggas in New York were hip to what went down in the clubs. Everybody came to chill and show off the latest gear. Guys came to meet girls and vice versa, but Brooklyn guys came to see what they could take and start trouble. Niggas from other boroughs knew the deal, and some came prepared for it. Some didn't.

"Dancing is for herbs," Tah continued.

Dawn was walking behind her boyfriend, who was walking toward Tah. Dawn looked frustrated to Mecca when he leaned and whispered in Tah's ear. Tah nodded. Dawn looked at Mecca with her arms folded and rolled her eyes. Tah and his partner started to walk off. Stopping briefly, Tah turned to Mecca.

"I'll see you in the ville."

With an anxious look on her face, Mecca yelled, "Where you going?"

Tah walked off. Walking over to Mecca, Dawn leaned to her ear and said, "They stupid, Mecca. They always starting something."

Mecca watched Tah and his crew walk to the exit and out of the club. The crowd seemed relieved. Five minutes later, Mecca and Dawn noticed some guys in the crowd talking to each other and hyperactively walking toward the exit. Then a bunch of girls and guys all headed toward the exit.

Mecca heard a girl tell another girl, "Something happened outside. It's probably them grimy-ass Brooklyn niggas!"

Mecca had a feeling whatever happened outside had Tah and his crew written all over it. Mecca grabbed Dawn and headed toward the exit. When they got in the front, a crowd gathered around someone lying on the ground. Mecca and Dawn broke through the crowd to see who the person was and what had happened to him.

"That's what niggas get when they try to rob somebody. Good for his ass!" Mecca and Dawn heard someone in the crowd yell out.

Dawn's legs gave out from under her when she saw her boyfriend laid out on the concrete with blood flowing out of his neck. He was making a gurgling sound. Dawn crawled to him as Mecca tried to hold her. Mecca looked up and down the block to see if she saw Tah or anybody in his crew, and they were nowhere to be found.

Ruby started second-guessing her decision to turn everything over to Mecca. Mecca was strong and could handle herself on the streets, but she had a weakness. A man. Ruby constantly told Mecca that a man would be her downfall. She introduced her to her Dominican connect in

Harlem. She told her connect that she was hot, and she told him about her arrest and the arrest of her workers.

"Don't worry, Ruby, my friend. Everything good for you. You beat the case," he responded in his thick Spanish accent. Ruby nodded grimly.

"Yeah, hopefully. Until then, I'm laying low. I'm going to let her run things until this shit is over. She knows what's what. This is my niece."

Ruby asked the Dominican for three kilos of cocaine on consignment so she could get things back in order. He told her to pick things up in two days. Back in Mecca's East New York apartment, Ruby gave Mecca instructions on how to run the show.

"Dawn is gonna have to manage all the spots for you. You're the boss now. You got to lay low. I'm going to give you the three pies, one for Coney Island, one for the ville, and the other for around here. Li'l Shamel got these cats around here in check. He's going to make sure these niggas do what they have to do. What's up with Dawn? You think she can handle this?" Ruby asked.

"Yeah, she knows what to do," Mecca replied.

Ruby's face turned sad. "I might have to do some time. Hopefully, this lawyer could get me a good plea or beat this shit. I'ma need you to hold shit down though, Mecca. You got to be strong. Don't let nothing slide. Don't show no weakness. The minute these niggas think that you going soft, they will be all over you like vultures. Somebody fuck up something small, treat it like it's big. These niggas y'all dealing with, don't let them in your business. Let them continue doing their own things. In fact, don't let them know nothing. The minute a nigga know you're doing better than him, his eyes will get in the way and cause serious problems."

Mecca nodded and soaked in everything Ruby said. She felt tears about to well up in her eyes at the thought of Ruby going to jail for a long time. Things wouldn't be the same without Ruby. She didn't know how she would be able to hold things down without her being around. She knew she had to do it, though, for Ruby and to prove to herself that she was a survivor. That night, Mecca decided to celebrate her new position, and she and Dawn headed to Union Square. Dawn would never be the same afterward.

The night Dawn's boyfriend was shot and killed at Union Square, Mecca was angry at Tah because it was their troublemaking that got Dawn's boyfriend, his partner, killed. Mecca decided she wouldn't talk to him for a few days. On the other hand, Dawn went to Brownsville Houses to confront Tah face to face.

"Why did y'all leave him?" Dawn yelled at Tah in an apartment rented by a crackhead Tah used as a hangout. Tah hugged Dawn, placing her head against his chest.

"Yo, we ain't know dude had a K-tone on him, Dawn. Son grabbed the nigga chain and yapped it before I could walk up. Then dude let off."

Dawn sobbed harder. "Why y'all gotta do that? Y'all got money! What y'all need a chain for?"

Tah couldn't answer that. He never thought of it like that. It's just the way he and his friends he grew up with were. *Dawn doesn't understand, it's the Brownsville way.*

Tah was caught off guard when Dawn grabbed his face and began kissing his lips. Tah kissed her back on her lips, at first gently, then their kissing became almost savage-like. They licked each other's faces then Tah pulled off his hooded sweatshirt.

Before either could make the conscious decision to stop and think about Mecca, Tah already had Dawn naked and there was no stopping them. In all honesty it felt so good they didn't want to stop, but after the act was over they both knew they had fucked up. Mecca was like Dawn's sister and she was Tah's girl. Trying to avoid eye contact as they got dressed, they both knew they would have to take their betrayal to the grave.

If Mecca ever found out what they had done, they would be in the grave a lot sooner than they would have liked to be. Without saying a word, Dawn left the house vowing to never get caught up with Tah like that again. Tah, on the other hand, knew he was wrong, but figured Dawn was weak and he could probably hit it again. As long as Mecca didn't know, they would be cool.

Mecca tried to block the vision of Dawn sucking Tah's dick out of her head, but she couldn't. She couldn't close her eyes to the vision because it was in her head.

"Why are you doing this to me?" Mecca yelled to Lou.

"You did this to yourself, Mecca. You chose this life. You made your bed. You ever heard the phrase 'life is what you make it'? Well, so is hell," Lou replied, laughing. "Ain't it hell watching your whole life recur?"

"Whatever point you tried to prove, you did it, okay?" Mecca yelled.

"Don't you wish you knew that your best friend was messing with your man, when you were alive?" Lou teased. "You would have killed her, right, Mecca?"

Mecca stood silent. She imagined herself finding out about Dawn and Tah. She envisioned herself walking in on them, pulling out a gun from her Coach bag, and shooting Tah first while Dawn watched in horror, then turning the gun on Dawn. She played the scene out in her head while Lou watched in amusement.

"Is he worth it, bitch? Is he?"

Dawn was crying and pleading, "I'm sorry, Mecca. I was just lonely after my boy died. Tah consoled me."

"You were lonely? Bitch, you know you could have come to me. You know what, fuck you, bitch!" Mecca pulled the trigger.

She snapped out of her vision when Lou said, "Betrayal hurts like hell, don't it? Trust me, I know how it feels. The creation of you human beings was a betrayal," Lou said, looking off in deep thought. "But that's another issue. Right now, Mecca, don't you wish you could start all over? Do you think you would do things different?"

Mecca held her head down with her eyes closed, shaking her head."What's the reason for all of this?" she asked.

Lou smiled while rubbing his palms together as if he were warming them. "I wouldn't use the word 'reason'," he said, putting his index finger up on his temple with his arms folded. "I would say . . ." Lou paused, going into deep thought, then, pointing his finger at Mecca, he concluded. "Purpose. The purpose for all of this."

"Well, what is the purpose?"

"I can show you better than I can tell you."

Chapter Twelve

Time waits for no man, can't turn back the hands, once it's too late, gotta learn to live with regrets.

Jay-Z

"I'm going uptown real quick, wait for me at your crib. I'ma bring those through. We are going to bag up in them tall caps. Go get them thirty ones illusion black tops," Ruby commanded Mecca over a pay phone on the corner of Bedford Avenue and Fulton Street

The corner was crowded with men and women dressed in the clothing of Arabs. The men and women weren't Arabs though. They were black men and women attending the mosque on the corner where Ruby used the pay phone. The smell of incense and oils permeated the sunny Bedford-Stuyvesant morning air.

While Ruby talked on the phone, she scanned the area up and down the street for any tails; police, or somebody trying to rob or kill her for something she did to her numerous victims. Fulton Street was a crowded street full of vendors selling T-shirts, children's and cultural books, and bootleg clothing and music, grocery stores, and guys hanging out hustling or looking for girls who paraded down one of the boroughs' main strips.

Ruby eyed almost everyone, thinking any of these people could be her killer. It was that way of thinking and paranoia that kept her alive as long as she had. Still it was impossible for her to see everybody, especially when that person was sitting in a burgundy Honda Accord with dark tinted windows watching her every move and following her.

"I'll be there in two hours. Don't go anywhere," Ruby concluded before hanging up. She got into her black Saab and drove down Fulton Street until she got to Flatbush Avenue. She turned on Flatbush Avenue and headed to the Manhattan Bridge. Ruby constantly checked her rearview mirror for any tail. The burgundy Honda Accord stayed three cars behind knowing where Ruby was headed.

She looked at her Bulova watch with gold numbers and hands against a black face. It was 9:30 a.m. She thought she'd be uptown by ten o'clock. She figured her connect would have her package by 10:45. *Them Dominican niggas be taking forever with the shit. I'll be in East New York by twelve o'clock.*

Ruby drove up the FDR Drive and got off at the 155th Street exit. She drove up to Eighth Avenue and went up to 155th Street. She pulled over, seeing her connect waiting on the corner. He smiled at Ruby as he got in. He was a skinny, dark-skinned Dominican cat. He wore a silk shirt opened at the chest, showing his multiple gold chains against his hairy chest. He reeked of cheap cologne, and his hair was slicked back. A midnight shadow adorned his face.

"Wassup, my friend?" he asked Ruby.

"What's up, Papi? Where we going?" Ruby asked driving slow.

Papi turned in his seat, looking out the back window. "Drive to the Bronx. It's hot around here. T.N.T. everywhere."

"The Bronx!" Ruby barked, frustrated. "Why all the way up there?"

"It's not far. It's right over the bridge," Papi countered.

Ruby sighed. No sense in arguing with him. Better safe than sorry. Ruby drove over the small bridge connecting the Bronx to Harlem. They drove a block away from Yankee Stadium, still being tailed by the burgundy Honda Accord, and pulled in front of a run-down tenement.

"Wait right here a few seconds. You got the money?" Papi asked.

If it were somebody else, Ruby would have killed him for asking for the money without showing the product. But she'd been dealing with him for years and they had a good repoire with each other. Ruby reached in the backseat and handed Papi a black Jansport book bag with $60,000 cash in it.

"You wait here. I come right back," Papi said, opening the door and jogging into the tenement. The area was also crowded with Spanish men on corners. Some were at small tables, playing dominoes and listening to salsa music. Women were hanging out of tenement windows looking at the men or watching their children play stickball in the streets.

The man in the Honda Accord fit right in with the neighborhood. He was a short Spanish man with a low haircut and a red Sergio Tacchini jogging suit. He slowly got out of the Accord while concealing behind his back a black .380

with a silencer on it. Ruby kept her eye on the tenement that Papi had gone into. Fortunately for her, a police cruiser stopped across the street from where she was parked. The driver of the Accord walked back to his car. Ruby, using her street smarts, drove off and didn't return. She drove back into Manhattan and the Spanish guy in the Accord followed. Ruby thought about the $60,000 she gave Papi, and decided she'd go back uptown tonight and meet him.

When Papi came out of the tenement, he saw the police car across the street and he walked to the corner store. He came out of the tenement without Ruby's Jansport. Ruby stopped at a pay phone on 125th and Eighth Avenue. Mecca picked up on the first ring.

"I'm going to be running late. It's hot. I had to get ghost for a minute. Just make sure you in the crib around eight o'clock tonight." Ruby hung up, paused, then dialed another number. After three rings a voice came over the line.

"Gilmore, Stein and Bloomberg, how may I assist you?" the secretary said in a squeaky voice, sounding as if she were holding her nose.

"I need to speak to Gilmore. Tell him it's Ruby Davidson."

"Hold on, Ms. Davidson." Ruby held on for what seemed like hours, listening to music that reminded her of the elevators she rode in when she went on a school trip to the Empire State Building as a kid.

"Ruby! What's up?" Gilmore said excitedly.

"Damn, you had me on hold long enough."

"Sorry about that. I was in a meeting with the partners. By the way, I got the discovery this morning. I need to go over some things with you. If you need a copy, I'll have my secretary do them now," Gilmore said wearily.

"I'll drop by and pick up the copies. I have to make some runs so we can discuss it tomorrow," Ruby said.

"All right, that'll be fine. I'll tell my secretary to have them ready. When can you stop by?" he asked.

"I'll be there in a half." Ruby hung up.

The Spanish guy driving the Accord watched Ruby from across the street while he ordered a hot dog from a vendor. With the crowds of people walking up and down and hanging around the world-renowned Harlem street with the famous Apollo Theater a few feet away, Ruby couldn't notice if anyone was following her. The Spanish guy kept a good distance between himself and Ruby when he knew where she was headed. Now that he had no idea where she was going, he played her a little closer than before.

A half hour later, Ruby picked up the copy of the govern-ment's evidence against her from Gilmore's secretary. The file was thick. There were hundreds of surveillance photos of Ruby and Stone getting into her Sterling in Brownsville. Stone's rap sheet was twenty pages long. There were mug shots of Ruby's workers in Brownsville and Coney Island.

Ruby was shocked to see a picture of her and her Dominican connect sitting in a Spanish restaurant on Amsterdam Avenue. There was a picture of Mecca in Langston Hughes and underneath the picture it said, "Davidson niece." There was a report on Mecca behind the picture. Ruby read the report.

Daughter of Bobby "Blast" Sykes and wife Mecca Sykes, who was killed in 1982 by masked men who invaded the home to rob Bobby Sykes of money and drugs. Present during the home invasion and murder of her parents, but couldn't identify the killers. Ruby Davidson took legal custody of her niece subsequently. G.I. Number 1 informs us that Mecca Sykes is not involved in her aunt's organization. This has to be investigated.

Ruby sighed as she parked on a side street in Midtown Manhattan reading the file. Before continuing to read, she took a sip of a Sprite she bought from a corner bodega. She turned to another page that had a picture of Dawn. Ruby spilled the Sprite on the car floor from the shock of what was written over Dawn's name. In bold, black print it said, "**G.I. NUMBER 1.**"

Blinded to what was going on in the street outside of the car, Ruby put the file on the passenger seat and reached down to get the soda can. The Spanish guy who drove the Accord exited his vehicle and sped toward her car. Ruby opened up the door and got out to wipe the car floor with a rag she took out of the glove compartment. The busy Manhattan day was buzzing with the sounds of loud talking, car horns, and trucks.

The Spanish guy approached from behind, but before he could raise his gun, Ruby spun around and pulled the trigger of her nickel-plated .45 that sent three bullets into the Spanish guy's face. The loud boom of the gun sent people on the streets running for cover. There were screams.

A police officer walking the beat saw Ruby standing over the Spanish guy, pumping three more bullets into his chest. Ducking down, she ripped the Spanish guy's pocket in his jogging suit and took a wad of bills. She picked up his gun and put it in her dark blue Fila velour pants and started walking back to her car.

"Lady, don't move! Drop the weapon and put your hands up!"

Ruby hesitated. She thought about Mecca. Her mind flashed back to when she was first born, when her sister had to get a C-section at Kings County Hospital. *What would Mecca do without me?* she thought. She had to tell Mecca about Dawn. She had to live. Ruby did as the cop ordered and dropped her weapon. Tears rolled down her face. She couldn't remember the last time she cried.

"Drop to your knees!" the cop yelled.

A crowd gathered around, looking at the dead Spanish guy with his blood flowing into the gutter. Cars stopped, blocking traffic, to see the bloody scene. The world seemed as if it were spinning to her. The cop's voice echoed in her ears.

"Put your hands above your head!"

Ruby put her hands behind her head and put her head down. She knew this was the end of her life of crime . . . at least on the streets.

"The Feds gave your aunt four life sentences and almost three hundred years and you still didn't get the message!" Lou barked at Mecca.

Mecca unfolded her arms and tried to turn her back on him, but everywhere she turned, Lou's image was in front of her.

"You didn't have to remind me," Mecca replied gravely. For the first time in her life Mecca felt like maybe she should have gotten out of the game earlier. Dawn had suggested it years ago, but now Mecca felt like she was a snake, too, and anyone she loved couldn't be trusted. Mecca was confused, and was trying to make sense of her life . . . the only life she knew how to live.

"Wow! Then your so-called best friend informed on her. Y'all call it snitching these days, ratting, whatever term y'all use. But you best friend? How much betrayal and loss of lives you've witnessed and experienced and you're not convinced that the life you were in wasn't worth all you went through?" Lou grinned as he spoke. Suddenly, he looked off to nowhere and spoke as if someone else was there with him and Mecca.

"I told you they would prove me right, Your Majesty," Lou yelled. Mecca looked around to see if she could see whom Lou was talking to, but saw nothing. "Why did I have to belittle myself for these beings who caused so much bloodshed and havoc among themselves? I deserve better," he screamed. Mecca had to hold her ears. In a split second Lou became calm again and turned back to her.

"Why did you have to kill Dawn? She didn't inform on you. She did what she did to save your life. To save you from the destructive life that your aunt, your own flesh and blood, led you to?"

"She did it to save her own ass."

"I beg to differ," Lou replied, snapping his fingers.

The snap made Mecca close her eyes and rub her temples as if she were suffering a migraine headache. An image appeared in her head. It was after Mecca received Dawn's photo with "G.I. Number 1" on it in the mail from Ruby.

Mecca, dressed in a blue Polo sweat suit and blue Reeboks, with her head wrapped in a blue bandanna scarf, held the papers in her hand as she and Dawn (dressed in a pair of hip-hugging, black Levi jeans, white Reeboks, and a white-button down Tommy Hilfiger shirt) sat on a bench in Brooklyn's Prospect Park on a late night.

Mecca waited almost a month after Ruby's letter, which simply said, "If you don't get rid of her, she will be your downfall. Remember, I told you before, don't let nothing slide." When Mecca gave Dawn the paper, Dawn reacted with shock and disbelief on her face.

"This ain't true, Mecca! I swear, I . . ." she cried. "You were at your aunt's hearing! I didn't testify against her at the hearing when the grand jury indicted her!"

Mecca thought, *this bitch must think I'm dumb.* They don't need her testimony at the grand jury! As Dawn spoke, Mecca looked around the park. It was dark except for the few streetlights that lined the walkways and streets that went through the park. Mecca chose a spot behind the trees and brush, blocking them from the view of people outside the park.

"Why would my aunt make this up? Why would she choose you to make this up on?" Mecca asked, beginning to feel the tears form in her eyes. She was in pain, hurt from the betrayal at the hands of her best friend, the only person she trusted besides her aunt. Dawn was like her sister and she had betrayed that trust. Mecca hated the position that she was in. The position the game forced her in. She couldn't walk away from this now. She had to hold it down for Ruby.

"Even if I did, Mecca, I would have done it for you. For you to get out of this game! But I didn't do—"

Before Dawn could finish her sentence, Mecca let off three shots to the chest, silencing her forever. It hurt because they had been through so much together, but then Mecca remembered that you couldn't trust anyone in the street. Especially someone that who supposed to be your family.

"You were a monster, Mecca!" Lou yelled as Mecca snapped out of the vision of shooting Dawn in the chest with a black .22 revolver, and afterward running out of the park, where Tah picked her up in his Porsche. Lou laughed. "I love it!"

Mecca looked at him confused. "Why is it so funny? I thought you didn't like what I was doing." Mecca said.

"I never said I liked it or didn't. I just find it hysterical and rather strange that"—Lou held his hands making quotation signs "God would create you human beings and allow you all to do these things to one another."

Mecca looked confused and finally asked, "Where am I? How long is this going to last?"

Lou grinned from ear to ear before giving an answer. Mecca had a dreaded feeling of what he was going to say, though she would have used a different term for "Eternity."

Chapter Thirteen

Everybody was making a lot of money. Within that year, Mecca's stash reached six kilos a week. Tah traded his '87 Porsche for the up-to-date one. Mecca copped the 1991 SL500, forest green with chrome Antera rims. Li'l Shamel copped a gold Land Cruiser and leased an apartment in the Sheepshead Bay section of Brooklyn.

Before Mecca made her move, she knew she had to get another connect once Ruby's connect was properly disposed of. Li'l Shamel was instrumental in providing Mecca with another connect. He introduced her to a Cuban cat he met on Rikers Island where he had been laid up for a few months for a gun charge before going "up north" to do a two-year sentence.

"This Cuban nigga got some shit, Mecca. He lives in Queens. They got that raw shit out there."

Mecca began to re-up from the Cuban who called himself "Heck," short for Hector. She wanted to establish a good rapport with Hector to be sure that she could trust him, because at the end of the day she didn't want to be totally assed out on a supplier. Tah, in the meantime, helped Mecca with her situation with the connect they would no longer be using. He had worked with him in the past, and knew this connect was always hungry for money.

"Papi, I need eight of them," Tah said on a pay phone in Brownsville Houses. Ruby's connect smiled on the other end of the phone as he stood on the corner of 156th and Amsterdam Avenue.

"Listen, Papi, I'm not trying to come uptown for it. It's been crazy hot up there lately. We can meet in Brooklyn; it ain't that hot out here like it is up there," Tah continued.

If it were someone else, Papi would have found the request truly out of line. Brooklyn wasn't the place a nigga in his right mind would bring three kilos of cocaine to sell to some nigga from out there. However, Papi trusted Tah because Tah made him a lot of money. He even gave Tah consignment and Tah brought him his money with no shorts. Tah even offered for Papi to come into business with him in Brooklyn. Papi thanked him for the offer, but he wanted no business dealings in the borough of crooks and killers. Papi asked Tah where he wanted to meet him after he agreed to coming to Brooklyn.

"Under the Brooklyn Bridge."

Papi showed up under the Brooklyn Bridge in a gold Lincoln Town Car, which was a cab driven by an old, fat, gray-haired Dominican man. To the surprise of everyone who lay in wait, Papi showed up by himself with no backup. He really trusted Tah. Niggas who ran with Tah didn't trust him, but Papi didn't know that Tah was from Brownsville, and was one of the neighborhood's most notorious stick up kids.

Not wanting to look suspicious, Papi wore a Yankee pinstriped jersey, tight blue jeans, and a pair of white Nike Air Max sneakers. Tah showed up in a Black Chevy Caprice with no hubcaps on the wheels; the crew's hooptie. The same one they used to go on missions with. He wore a sky blue Nautica sweat suit with a pair of white and sky blue canvas Air Force Ones.

Tah got out of the car with a black duffel bag. Papi carried a large brown paper bag that had the words in big print on it, "BIG BROWN BAG." He walked over to the Lincoln town car that parked behind the Caprice under the Bridge. The streets were empty on the cloudy day. The smell of garbage and human waste was strong here.

When he reached the destination he placed the duffel bag on the trunk of the town car. Tah and Papi turned quickly, hearing footsteps and the sound of metal smacking into metal. They saw a homeless man pushing a shopping cart filled with soda cans. The homeless man had a long, beige, filthy trench coat, and a dirty, red, yellow, and green wool Jamaican hat. He walked with his head down.

He picked up a can on the ground and threw it in the shopping cart, taking a short glance at Tah and Papi. Tah waived off the homeless man, and Papi turned back to him and put the brown paper bag on the trunk. Tah looked in and saw the eight kilos of cocaine tightly wrapped with duct tape.

Tah and Papi heard the footsteps of the homeless man stop behind them. When they turned to look, the homeless man was picking up a small brown paper bag that had something in it. The homeless man looked in the bag curiously. They turned their attention away from the bum again and didn't see him pull a .25-caliber automatic out of the bag.

The old man in the Lincoln looked at the homeless man and his eyes widened in shock when he saw the gun. "Mira Carlos!" the driver yelled, trying to warn them that the man had a gun.

The homeless man put two bullets in the back of Papi's head. Tah reached in his pocket, pulled out his .380 automatic, ran to the driver's side of the Lincoln, and pumped five bullets into the old cab driver's head and neck.

Tah and the homeless man jumped in Tah's Caprice and sped off. Two members of Tah's crew parked down the block in a blue Acura Integra saw Tah pull out from under the bridge, and they pulled out after Tah and the homeless man drove by them.

"You can take the hat and that nasty-ass coat off. That shit stinks." Tah snorted. When the homeless man took the hat and coat off, Tah smiled at the person who wasn't a man, but his pretty girlfriend, Mecca.

Tah stopped the car in front of an apartment building that had a green dumpster in the alley. He grabbed Mecca's homeless costume and the duffel bag filled with newspaper and tossed it in the dumpster. He jumped back in the car and with the tires screeching, he sped off.

Chapter Fourteen

Lust not after her beauty in thine heart, neither let her take thee with her eyelids.

Proverbs 6:2

Li'l Shamel, actually Shamel Jacobs, was twenty-one years old in 1995 like Mecca. He got his name from Ruby. No one called him that except her. He never knew why Ruby called him that, but he always thought it was a joke because for his age he was built like a thirty-year-old running back.

During his time in juvenile and adult prisons throughout New York, Shamel did nothing but read books and work out. He had been in and out of group homes and jails all of his life. The coppertoned, wavy-haired, hazel-eyed Shamel was born and raised in the East New York section of Brooklyn. His mother and father were alcoholics who lived in Cypress projects. He grew tired of their alcohol-induced abuse on him physically, as well as watching his father beat on his mother, so he chose to stay with his grandmother in Sutter Gardens.

Sutter Gardens was a two-story housing complex that was a little cleaner and less dangerous than Cypress projects where Shamel had lived with his parents. But Sutter Gardens was far from safe. Already trained and equipped to brawl, Shamel had to prove himself the same way he did in Cypress, and he did. Shamel never lost a fight in Sutter Gardens and he gained the respect from the neighborhood tough guys by beating all of them one by one. Shamel always said he was no "stranger to danger," and adjusted well to the change that took place in the streets once crack hit the hood. That danger was guns.

Shamel got his first gun when he was fourteen years old. It was a .38 Special he found in a vacant lot where he and a few guys from the hood stashed their packages of crack. The first time he used it was when he was fifteen. He went to Empire Roller Skating Rink in Crown Heights strapped with his .38. When he and a friend got to the rink there was a group of guys from the Heights Ebbets Field projects in the front and they didn't look like they just came to skate and have a good time. They looked like trouble.

Shamel wore a black Woolrich coat, and a black Champion hooded sweater with a pair of black Girbaud jeans and a white and gray pair of New Balance sneakers. He had a gold nugget watch on his wrist and the watch caught the attention of the Ebbets Field crew. Shamel's friend held the .38 in his beige Woolrich. There was a crowd of mostly females waiting to get in the roller rink and cars blasting music were pulling up in front trying to find parking. The music blasted from the inside of the rink so it was hard for Shamel and his friend to hear one of the guys say for him to give up his jewelry.

"Yo, money, run that watch!" Shamel and his friend kept walking and that angered the Ebbets Field guys.

"Yo, duke! You ain't hear me? Run that watch!" one of the guys ran up and yelled in front of Shamel and his friend. Shamel looked the guy up and down, noticing he didn't have a weapon in his hand. Shamel turned to look at the other guys and none of them had any weapons.

"What you say?" he asked.

"Nigga, run that watch," the guy yelled again, this time getting more pissed off.

Shamel looked at his friend who gave Shamel the "What you wanna do?" look. Shamel smiled at his friends who were still looking at the dude.

“I’ma give duke the watch, so we can bounce!” Shamel took the watch off and handed it to the guy who was smiling at his crew behind Shamel.

“Y’all good?” Shamel asked. “We ain’t got no money,” Shamel lied, tapping his pocket.

“Get the fuck outta here, pussy,” the guy with the watch said while putting it on his wrist. Shamel and his friend took a couple of steps past the guy who was admiring the Rolex with his crew standing around him.

“Pass me the biscuit, son,” Shamel whispered to his friend. His friend slowly pulled it out of his jacket and handed it to Shamel.

The Ebbets Field crew had their backs to Shamel. Shamel turned around and walked up behind the guy with the watch. The music blocked them from hearing his approach. It was dark outside except for the light around the skating rink.

Shamel placed the gun to the neck of the guy with the watch and squeezed the trigger. The loud boom and seeing their partner fall face-forward made the Ebbets Field crew take off like a flock of pigeons flying off when someone approaches. Being that Empire Roller Rink was down the block from where Shamel shot the guy, the line of people in front of Empire did not hear or see him shoot, then take his watch off of the now dead guy's wrist. Still standing over the guy, Shamel put his watch back on after tucking the gun in his coat pocket. He walked over to his friend and with no show of emotion they kept on with their night as planned.

"There's mad bitches in that joint. Let's go."

His friend shook his head. "You crazy, son."

From that point on, Shamel did not hesitate to pull the trigger on anybody who even slightly disrespected him or any of his friends. He caught his first body when he went to Cypress to visit his mother. The Ebbets Field guy didn't die; he was paralyzed from the neck down. When he got to his mother's apartment, he heard her screams from the hallway.

"Stop, Brian, you're hurting me!"

When he entered the apartment, his mother's face and naked body had blood and bruises, old and new, all over them. Shamel's father was standing over his mother—who was curled up on the couch covered with a dirty fitted sheet stained with alcohol and piss--with a two-by-four of plywood in his hand. Shamel immediately reached for the .38 he had on his waist and without saying a word he emptied all six shots into his father's head and body. When his father slumped to the dirty, brown carpet, his mother jumped off the couch on top of her husband and cried.

"Baby, no! Don't die, baby! He didn't mean it!" Shamel's mother cried while cradling his dead father's body. She looked up at Shamel with tears flowing down her face.

"Why you do that, you mu'fucka!"

Shamel realized his mother was drunk and decided he'd come back when she was sober. He left and went home to his grandmother, not even bothering to answer, and left her there, drunk and crying.

"Grandma, what's wrong?" he asked, hugging her. Her entire body was shaking like a leaf.

"Baby, your mamma called the police on you! She said you killed your daddy."

"She called the police?" Shamel asked, holding his grandmother at arm's length.

"Baby, you gotta go somewhere because she told them you're here!" She nodded, pushing him toward the door. Shamel never made it out of Sutter Gardens.

The police were all over the place when he stepped outside. He gave up with no incident. He was a juvenile at the time and the courts were lenient because Shamel was emotionally distressed when he saw his mother being abused. He was given eighteen months in a juvenile lockup in upstate New York.

Ruby and Mecca took a liking to Shamel. He was loyal and he was about making money. He treated Mecca like a sister and when cats in Sutter Gardens tried to approach her to get some play, Shamel would quickly scold the offender verbally and sometimes physically. After a while no guy in Sutter Gardens came within two feet of her.

Secretly, Shamel had the biggest crush on Mecca. Even though she thought Shamel was good looking and he was a "real nigga," she loved Tah, and off the strength of Mecca, Shamel showed Tah love when he came to East New York, even though East New York guys and Brownsville guys didn't get along.

Mecca suspected Shamel had a crush on her when her twenty-first birthday came around; Shamel bought Mecca a pair of Channel boots and a five-karat tennis bracelet. Then to put the icing on the cake, he threw a surprise pool party for her at the Paedergat in Canarsie. All the hustlers from Coney Island, Brownsville, and East New York attended.

When Mecca showed up, Shamel had a red carpet rolled out for her. She was impressed and at the same time sad because Tah never did anything like that for her. His birthday gifts were predictable. He would buy her a pocketbook, take her to the movies and an expensive restaurant, then to the Waldorf or Plaza Hotel to spend a weekend having sex.

When Mecca arrived in her SL300, Shamel opened the door for her and walked her down the red carpet. He had one of his soldiers throw rose petals at her feet as she walked. She wore a full-length white mink over a white linen, one-piece dress by Giorgio Armani. The black, Gucci, five-inch-heeled shoes matched the black handbag by Christian Dior perfectly.

"Damn, Mecca, you're a star!" Shamel told her as she walked in.

"You look damn good yourself!" Mecca smiled, holding on to Shamel's arm. He wore a white linen suit by Armani, and a black Bossalini with a white silk band around it. On his feet, he matched the hat with a pair of black gators with a gold buckle. He adorned his wrist with an oyster perpetual Rolex with diamonds on the bezel and a four-karat pinky ring with a platinum setting. As they entered the pool area, where no one was because no one came dressed to get in a pool, Shamel looked around as if looking for someone in particular.

"Where your boy at?" Shamel asked.

"Who, Tah? Please, that nigga found it more important to be out of town than to be here for my birthday," Mecca replied, looking at the ballers and girls who showed up at her party. She recognized some of the guys from Brownsville and Coney Island, but the guys from East New York she didn't know personally. She knew who some of them were by face and reputation. Most of them were infamous stick up men who took down some of the biggest drug dealers in the city. Shamel knew all of them and they respected him. He impressed Mecca to the fullest extent when the big-name guys sent him over bottles of Cristal and some hugged him as he went by while wishing Mecca a happy birthday.

Shamel spent the whole night with her. He danced with her fast and slow. When Mary J Blige's "I Never Wanna Live Without You" song from her *My Life* album came on, Shamel hugged Mecca real tight while they slow danced. Mecca could hear his heart beat as she rested her head on his chest. His muscular chest felt good to Mecca and she wondered what he looked like naked.

What kind of nigga would be out of town for his girl's birthday? Especially a girl like Mecca? This nigga must not realize what he got. She is a bad mu'fucka, and her body is off the hook. To top it off, she a soldier! A nigga couldn't ask for better, Shamel thought.

The surprise Shamel had for Mecca didn't end at the pool party. He and his East New York crew all chipped in and copped Mecca a candy-apple red Lexus GS400. When he pulled up in front of his building, the Lexus was parked in front with a red ribbon around it.

It was four o'clock in the morning, and the crew was supposed to be there as part of the surprise, but they got tired and took off for the night. Still in all, Shamel pointed to the car and said, "Happy birthday, Mecca. That right there is yours."

Even though Mecca could afford to buy the Lexus herself, the thought that Shamel would go this far for her birthday made tears well up in her eyes. She hugged Shamel tight.

"Thank you, Shamel. Why you doing all of this?" Mecca asked, a little confused and hating that he wasn't her man. Shamel held Mecca back so he could look in her eyes. Mecca looked at him and thought this nigga looked real good.

"'Cause you deserve it. You and your aunt are like the family I wished for." Shamel looked away from Mecca out the front window of the car. "I don't understand how this nigga ain't around for your birthday. You deserve better, Mecca."

Mecca thought about what Shamel said all night. When Tah's birthday came, Mecca went all out to make his birthdays unforgettable. She cooked big dinners for him and his crew, and gave him the best sex he could ever come by, and he had the nerve to not even be around for hers.

"What's better, Shamel?" she asked, grinning. Shamel hopped out of the driver's seat, walked around and opened the door for her, and grabbed her hand.

"C'mon with me."

"Where are we going?" she asked as she held his hand.

"My crib. I wanna show you something."

"Ain't we going to wake your grandmother up?" Mecca asked, but didn't hesitate to follow him. Shamel kept holding her hand while walking to his building.

"My grandmother went down south two days ago."

Mecca had been inside Shamel's house before, usually to drop off packages for him to give the workers. She gave him consignment. If she picked up six keys, she would give Shamel two and charge him twenty thousand. She would profit two thousand off of each key.

Every time she came to his crib, he fought the urge not to make a move on her. His rationale was that he didn't want to put her in an uncomfortable situation with Tah. Shamel also didn't want to ruin their friendship and business venture. He figured he'd just wait until Tah fucked up. Now the opportunity presented itself and he wasted no time making the move he had wanted to make since the first day he laid eyes on her.

When he and Mecca entered the apartment, Shamel cut the light on and the nicely decorated two-bedroom apartment came into view with the smell of potpourri in the air. He got right down to business.

He held Mecca's face between his palms. She looked at him confused until he put his lips to hers and parted her mouth with his tongue. For a moment she hesitated, then gave into his advances. The kiss was sensual and Mecca felt the wetness begin to develop between her thighs. She acknowledged to herself that this nigga could kiss and his lips were soft. For the first time, she didn't have to taste cigarettes in her mouth. Shamel didn't smoke, while Tah smoked like a Navajo Indian.

Shamel lifted Mecca up with ease and carried her into his bedroom that had a queen-sized bed, a fifty-inch Sony television, a surround sound system along its side, and a *Ms. Pacman* arcade game in the corner with stacks of sneaker boxes lined up on the wall beside it.

Posters of the Notorious B.I.G. were everywhere along with pictures of guns torn out of a *Guns & Ammo* magazine. There were clothes thrown on a folded metal chair in front of his closet.

His strength turned her on. He made her feel special. She felt like a princess. Tah never carried her into the bedroom. The sex with Tah was good, but Tah was the only person she ever had sex with, so how would she know the sex was good when she never experienced sex with anyone else? This was her opportunity to find out if Tah's sex was indeed good.

She was surprised at her own feelings. The thought of giving herself to another man usually made her feel guilty, but for some reason she didn't feel that way with Shamel. Maybe it was because he showed her more attention in one night than Tah did in five years. On that note, she gave her full attention to Shamel and was willing to do whatever Shamel wanted to do in bed.

Shamel kissed Mecca softly on her neck, which made chills run through her whole body. He nibbled on her ear lobe. It tickled Mecca a bit, but she still moaned with a small chuckle. At the same time, he let his hand slip up her dress and rub her vagina outside of her laced Victoria's Secret panties. Mecca arched her back and inhaled deeply.

He felt the wetness of her on her panties. Slowly he slid her panties down while he kissed her on her lips. He lifted her dress up to her waist, got on his knees and removed her shoes, sucking her toes. Tah never sucked on Mecca's toes, and Mecca didn't know getting her toes sucked would feel so good.

While he did that, she lifted the dress over her head and threw it on the floor. She removed her bra while looking at Shamel suck each toe individually. He licked her ankles, then her calves slowly. Then he kissed her inner thighs until he buried his face between her legs. He opened her pussy lips with his thumbs and sucked on her clitoris. Mecca felt his warm tongue on her and almost flipped off the bed. She gripped the sheets as she came all over Shamel's face.

"Shamel, don't stop! Oh Shamel, keep eating my pussy," she moaned.

Shamel ate Mecca's pussy for a half hour. Mecca came more times in that half hour than she did in a month with Tah. When he finished, his face looked like a glazed donut.

"You taste so good, Mecca," Shamel said seductively. He took off his linen suit and stripped naked down to his silk socks.

Mecca had fantasized about Shamel's body before. When his Sutter Garden basketball team played against other teams, most from other parts of East New York in high-stakes games, Mecca stared at the bulge in his shorts. Seeing him naked, she found that what she fantasized about was actually the way she pictured it. Along with his chiseled muscular frame, he had the biggest dick Mecca could have ever imagined. She thought Tah's dick was good to go, but damn. Shamel was holding!

She was almost scared. Before she let him stick his pole in her pussy, Mecca wanted to return the oral favor. She got up and pushed Shamel on the bed on his back. She wiped her juices off his face with her hands then she stuck her tongue in his mouth and they kissed for a few seconds. She sucked on his nipples and Shamel closed his eyes. His heart was beating fast. He couldn't believe he finally got the girl he always wanted, and she felt the way he imagined she would. He got to make love to her the way he pictured when he masturbated with her in mind.

Shamel didn't feel it was the right time to reveal to Mecca how he felt. He knew time would tell how she felt about him. He knew telling her that he had once had rough sex with her aunt Ruby back in the day would make him telling her he loved her unbelievable. He would never tell her that though, and hopefully, Ruby wouldn't either.

Shamel moaned as Mecca went south, gripping his dick. He could feel her tongue massaging his shaft while her lips moved up and down his dick. She massaged his balls while she sucked and Shamel started humping her mouth. At first Mecca gagged, then she handled all of him like a pro. Shamel held Mecca's head, stopping her.

"I wanna cum in you, Mecca, not in your mouth."

Mecca smiled. "We got enough time for that. You tasted me, so gimme a chance to taste you."

Shamel stalled and leaned his head back. In between the sound of Mecca slurping on his manhood, he felt himself about to explode. Mecca felt his hot cum splash against the back of her throat. She kept sucking as his juices flowed down her throat. Shamel gripped the bed and lifted his waist.

"Damn, girl, oh shit," he moaned, looking at her while she was licking the cum off the tip of his dick.

"You good?" Mecca looked at him, smiling.

Shamel laughed, "No doubt, baby girl."

Mecca began to stroke Shamel's dick to get it hard again. She rubbed her palms to warm them, then started playing with his balls. "C'mon, big boy, get up," she said, looking at his semi-erect dick. She licked the head of Shamel's dick and it stood at full attention, hard and ready in no time. Mecca crawled on her knees, smiling seductively at him.

"Come here," he said, folding the pillow under his head lifting it.

Mecca climbed on top of him, reached behind, and grabbed his dick. She lifted herself and slowly slid down on him. She inhaled deeply and screwed up her face, feeling Shamel's dick fill her insides. Shamel palmed both of her plump ass cheeks while she leaned forward so he could suck on her light brown breasts with the dark brown nipples.

She rode his dick in a slow rhythm. Every time she moved, Shamel felt his dick tingle with pleasure. He fought back the urge of moaning out loud, and whispered, "Damn this pussy good. I want you, Mecca, all to myself!"

"You got me, oh God, you got me," Mecca responded in between moans, savoring the feel of his dick beating on her G-spot while she bounced up and down on the entire length of him.

Shamel turned Mecca doggie style, held her by her waist, and watched his dick go in and out of her dark pink pussy surrounded by golden brown skin and curly pubic hairs. He slapped her ass, sending chills through Mecca's body. Mecca moaned with every stroke and slap on her ass.

Shamel held her shoulders while he pumped, looking at her flawless skin. Her ass was smooth like a baby's ass. She turned her head, looking at him as he pumped. Her face was turning red and she held her mouth open.

"Oh, Shamel, fuck this pussy! Fuck me."

He pushed Mecca down so her stomach could touch the bed. He lifted her ass up and pushed himself deeper in her. Mecca felt herself cumming and it didn't stop. Her whole body shook as she came all over Shamel's dick. Cum dripped down her legs from her pussy.

After ten minutes in that position, he laid her on her back and put her legs over his shoulders. Mecca came three times before Shamel bust his second nut. Mecca felt his cum inside her and she pulled his waist into her.

Mecca and Shamel fell asleep in each other's arms. She woke up first and snuck into the kitchen to cook breakfast in bed at three o'clock in the afternoon. Forty-five minutes later, Mecca woke Shamel up with a steaming plate of French toast, scrambled cheese eggs, and home fries, with a glass of milk and orange juice.

"Damn, you can cook, too? That nigga Tah is crazy," Shamel said as he leaned his back against the wooden headboard while Mecca dressed in one of his T-shirts with nothing else on. She placed his plate on a pillow and set the pillow on his lap. Mecca went back into the kitchen and grabbed her plate, and went back in the room with Shamel and sat on the bed next to him.

"Speaking of that nigga, he has been beeping me all morn-ing," Mecca said, grabbing her clear pink pager off the nightstand next to the bed.

"Where he beeping you from?"

"The area code is seven-one-seven. That's in Pennsylvania somewhere," she replied, putting the pager down on the stand.

"You should call. Something might be wrong," Shamel said.

Even though he wanted Mecca for himself, and Tah out of the way, he knew that still didn't mean he could totally shit on the nigga. He might have been in jail, and Shamel didn't wish that on anybody. He wasn't about to go to war with no dude about his girl. He knew, regardless if it was Mecca, nothing was worth your freedom, and he refused to die over a woman.

Shamel handed Mecca his gray Motorola cellular phone. Mecca looked at her pager while she dialed the number. A voice answered on the first ring.

"Harrisburg Police Department. How may I help you?"

"Sorry, I dialed the wrong number," Mecca said, quickly hanging up. She looked at Shamel with her eyebrow raised. "That was the police in Harrisburg. I think that nigga locked up."

"Why you hang up?" Shamel asked.

"He might be under a fake name. I gotta call the ville and see what's what," Mecca answered. Mecca dialed another number, then pressed the send button on the cellular phone.

Chapter Fifteen

The labeling of a snitch is a lifetime scar/
You'll always be in jail . . . minus the bars.
Jay-Z

Knowing it wasn't a wise move discussing the specifics over the phone of why Tah was locked up, Mecca decided to drive to Brownsville to get the full details on the goings-on that got Tah caged in Pennsylvania. She drove to the ville in her new Lexus. When she pulled up in the Brownsville Houses in the bright red Lexus, all eyes were on her. She spotted some of Tah's crew standing in front of his building. They stared at the car, not knowing who was driving.

When Mecca stopped and got out, she could see the crew mumbling to each other. Other people went back to their business while a group of girls with bad hairdos and cheap, ten-dollar dresses rolled their eyes and stared at Mecca enviously. Mecca called over one of the crew.

"Craig, come here." Craig, a short, purple-black-complexioned cat with a bald head dressed in camouflage fatigues and construction Timbs skipped over to Mecca.

"What's up?" he asked, showing his chipped tooth and bottom teeth in gold with engraved letters saying "C-Money."

"What happened to Tah?"

Craig shook his head and sighed. "I told that nigga don't go down there with scary-ass Mika. He had to clap one of them Pennsylvania niggas, and both the dude and Mika told he did it. Now he locked up with a hundred grand bail."

"Mika? You talking about Tamika with the scar on her face that he used to fuck with back in the day?" Mecca asked, surprised.

"Yeah, that Mika," Craig said.

Mecca was about to ask a thousand questions in regard to Tamika and Tah's dealing with each other, but there was no need in asking Craig because he would lie for Tah anyway. Mecca knew she had to ask him face to face.

"They got that ten percent shit down there. All he need is ten Gs," Craig said, snapping Mecca out of the thought of Tah dealing with Tamika behind her back. Mecca walked back to the car and opened the passenger-side door, reached in the glove compartment, and pulled out a blue and white Gap bag. She handed the bag to Craig.

"That's eleven; go get the nigga."

Tah showed up at Mecca's apartment the next day wearing a brown Pelle Pelle leather jacket and black Parasuco jeans, with brown and green Gore-Tex Timbs known as "beef & broccolis."

"Yo, good-looking, boo! I had to get outta there, they be hanging niggas out there, for real!" Tah said, sitting down on Mecca's couch. Mecca rolled her eyes with a look that seemed to Tah like she wasn't happy to see him.

"What's up with you? Ain't you glad to see me?" Tah asked with his palms held out, shrugging his shoulders.

Mecca sucked her teeth. "Please, nigga, if I didn't want to see you I wouldn't have bailed your dumb ass out. What the fuck were you doing with Tamika?"

Tah put his hands on his lap and screwed up his face. "Who told you I was with Mika? Niggas got big mouths and don't be knowing what they talking about."

Mecca stood in front of him with her hands on her hips. "Niggas was talking about what happened to you and how you got locked up, stupid. How the hell else I was going to bail your dumb ass out?" Mecca shot back. "You in Pennsylvania with Tamika instead of with me on my birthday, huh?"

"It ain't even like that, Mecca. Don't go jumping to conclusions," Tah said, knowing how heated Mecca could get in no time. He didn't feel like her bullshit because he knew they would argue for the rest of the night.

"Like what, Tah? Fuck is you talking about? You weren't here with me, that's the conclusion."

"You saying it like I'm fuckin' her or something. That bitch a mule."

"So, what you was mule dicking her?" Mecca said sarcastically.

Tah sighed, not wanting to continue arguing about Tamika. He felt stupid even dealing with her again sexually and bringing her out of town with coke in her bra, girdle, and pussy. It was this bitch's fault he got locked up.

A guy from Harrisburg approached Tamika in a bar and asked her name. Instead of saying her name then politely telling the guy she had a man, she said, "Don't worry what my name is. Get your country ass out my face!"

The guy slapped the taste out of Tamika's mouth. She held her face then started swinging on the guy. Tah walked in the bar and saw the guy and Tamika throwing blows at each other.

Tah ran over and tried to pull Tamika away. The guy kept swinging and mistakenly punched Tah in the face. Tah let go of Tamika, pulled a .45 from his pants, and shot the guy in his stomach and arm.

The bar cleared in panic. Tah and Tamika took off running toward the hotel they were staying in, but they didn't make it back to the hotel. The cops caught them three blocks from the bar. They had the ambulance with the shot guy in it come to where they stopped Tah and Tamika. Before the ambulance pulled up, Tamika started running her mouth.

"Officer, I ain't do nothing. I ain't shoot nobody. I ain't tell him to shoot him!"

Tah tried to tell her to shut up, but she kept yapping. They opened the back of the ambulance where the guy lay on a stretcher, holding his stomach, pointing at Tah.

"Please, Mecca. I ain't fucking her. I don't want to argue about this no more. I'm sorry I wasn't here for your birthday, and I'll make it up to you. I got to pick up some money first."

"I know you're going to run and get my ten Gs back," Mecca said while walking away.

"All right. A yo, who Lexus is that in front of the crib?" Tah asked, walking over to the window and moving the black curtains to look at it.

"It's mine. It was a birthday gift!" Mecca yelled from the kitchen.

"Damn, who gave you that for your birthday?" Tah asked curiously.

"Shamel and his crew chipped in and copped it for me!"

Tah felt the anger build up in his chest jealously. "Word? Niggas feeling you like that?"

Mecca walked back in the living room with her hand on her hip. "Please, Tah. At least niggas thought about me on my birthday. Niggas ain't trying to get with me. Niggas is family. Niggas is loyal."

Mecca lied about Shamel, but she told the truth about the other guys not wanting to get with her. Tah got up and walked toward the door.

"Where you going?"

Tah opened to door and without looking at her, he answered, "I'm going to get your money." Then, slammed the door.

Tamika walked around Brownsville like she had no worries. At first she figured Tah loved her and wouldn't hurt her. Plus, he was out of jail, and she knew Tah didn't expect her to take the fall for the shooting. She already brought drugs out there for him, what else did he expect? All of those thoughts changed when she realized he was avoiding her. She tried to speak to him on the phone. She tried beeping him and calling his cellular phone but when he heard her voice, he hung up. He erased her number off his beeper and told a group of her girlfriends to tell Mika she didn't exist to him anymore.

Then Mika stepped over the line when she went to Sutter Gardens and knocked on Mecca's door. Luckily for Tamika, Mecca wasn't home, but her emotions superseded her intelligence. She wrote on Mecca's door in black marker, *Tah, I'm sorry. I didn't mean to hurt you. I love you.* She could never catch Tah at home, so she knew for sure that he would see her note at Mecca's house.

Mecca was usually out of the city staying at Ruby's villa, which Mecca owned legally. The house was in her name and her SSI savings covered the mortgage. Ruby's lawyer helped Mecca secure the home. She happened to be in the city often since she and Shamel started creeping around. Tah spent most of the time in Brownsville doing stick ups and hanging with his crew.

He went to see Mecca twice a week, either to drop off money or spend a night after having boring sex. After the wonderful sex Mecca was having with Shamel, she seemed disinterested when she had sex with Tah. The sex she had with

Shamel was always satisfying and they never did the same things. There was always something new when they got together. Mecca came to her apartment after spending time with Shamel and saw what Tamika wrote on her door.

"Oh no, this bitch didn't!" Mecca grumbled, opening her door. She picked up her phone and called Shamel. "Boo, you won't guess what this bitch Tamika did to my door!"

Shamel rushed over to Mecca's Brownsville apartment to see what was going on. Shamel was shocked when he saw it and he knew that whoever this Tamika was, she done fucked up. He thought if he knew Tamika, he would have told her, "You don't wanna do that. Mecca is not the one."

"This bitch doesn't learn, huh? I cut this bitch face in school and she still don't get it!" Mecca said angrily. "C'mon Shamel, we going to find this bitch!"

Mecca drove her Benz with Shamel riding shotgun with the seat leaned all the way back. Mecca drove with her seat leaned back so far it looked like the car was driving by itself, if you looked from the outside.

Both of them had their guns on them. Mecca had a chrome .45 with a pearl handle that Shamel bought off a crackhead for her. Shamel had a

MAC-11 with a shoestring tied around it that he put on his shoulder under his red and gold Avirex leather jacket. Mecca saw Tah and his crew standing on the corner of Mother Gaston and Dumont and pulled up on the corner. She walked straight over to Tah.

Tah saw the anger on her face and mumbled to his crew, "Now what?" Shamel got out of the car with her and that angered him even more.

"Where's that nappy headed-bitch of yours, Tah?" Mecca yelled.

"What is you talking 'bout, Mecca? What bitch?" Tah, asked confused.

"Don't play stupid! Tell the bitch she can tell you she love you in your face or on a postcard, not on my fucking door!"

"Fuck is you talking about?" Tah asked, then he pointed at Shamel. "Fuck is he doing here? He your bodyguard now?"

Shamel interjected, "Hold up, son. Mecca is my peoples. I'm holding her down. Ain't nobody trying to take what's yours. So leave me outta this, kid."

Tah looked Shamel up and down menacingly and so did Tah's crew, who began mumbling under their breath. Mecca pulled out her gun and cocked it. Tah's crew all pulled out their guns when Mecca brandished hers.

"Ain't nobody gonna front on my peoples. So y'all niggas don't even think about it!"

"Y'all niggas chill!" Tah yelled to his crew. He turned to Mecca. "Mecca, put the biscuit away, ain't nobody gonna do nothing." Tah smiled at Shamel. "I don't know what you did, son, but whatever it is, put me on, 'cause I doubt if she'll do that for me."

Shamel ignored Tah's sarcasm. "Son, she bailed you out as soon as she heard you got locked up, and . . ." He figured he should cap it off with what he knew was somewhat true. "She love you, son, you're all she talks about when she in the East."

Tah looked at Mecca, and then he reached out to hug her. Mecca pulled back. "Where's this bitch? She wrote on my door, Tah. She must think you live there or she lost her mu'fuckin' mind!"

"Mecca, I don't fuck with that bitch. Why would I fuck with a bitch who snitched on me?" Mecca started walking back to her car with Shamel in tow. Tah stood there with his crew, angry."I'm saying, where you going, Mecca? Let me talk to you!"

Mecca looked back at Tah with the "yeah, right" look on her face."Talk to that bitch of yours, because I ain't doing no talking."

Mecca drove around Brownsville looking for Tamika. Crews of guys hanging out on corners stared as Mecca drove down Rockaway Avenue and Mother Gaston Boulevard. Girls stared with envy when they realized it was a girl driving. Some recognized Mecca from going to school with her. Some of them waved to Shamel out of spite, which Mecca ignored. Mecca noticed Shamel shake his head when the girls waved at him.

"I'd rather die than be like them bitches," Mecca said.

"I feel you on that."

Shamel noticed Mecca's eyes widen when she looked at another group of girls on the corner of Pitkin and Belmont.

"There go that bum-ass bitch right there!" Mecca pointed.

Shamel looked at the group. "What you wanna do?"

Mecca pulled over."This bitch ain't worth killing, I'll beat her ass." She put her gun in the glove compartment. "Just hold me down just in case these bitches try to front," Mecca continued.

"No question," Shamel replied.

They both got out of the car. Tamika saw Mecca coming and shock was all over her face. Tamika could have pissed her pants at the sight of her nemesis. The girl who cut her face back in junior high. The girl who took her man. Yet, Tamika had to save face in front of her crew, so she initiated the standoff.

"Bitch, you walking over here like you—" Tamika was cut off by the sound of Mecca's fist against her jaw. Mecca kept swinging and punching Tamika in her face. She tried to fight back.

"Bitch, don't you ever come to my crib." Mecca spoke after each punch. "Looking for Tah. You bum-ass bitch!"

Mecca held Tamika's head down with one hand and uppercut her in the face with the other. Tamika's nose was bleeding and her jaw was dangling from Mecca breaking it with her first punch. Tamika's friends were yelling at Tamika.

"Mika, beat her ass! Don't let her do that to you!"

One of them even tried to grab Mecca. Shamel held his hand out in front of the girl while putting one hand in his jacket. "Get the fuck back before I pistol whip one of you bitches!"

The girls saw the menacing look Shamel gave and backed up.

"That's it, Mecca, damn, you got it!"

Mecca threw Tamika on the ground and saw that a large crowd was watching. Most of them were shopping on the busy strip of Pitkin Avenue. Some people stood at bus stops watching the girls. Groups of guys watched to see if one of the girls' clothes were ripped off to get a flash.

Chunks of Tamika's extensions came out of her hair. Her tight blue Guess jeans had dirt on them from the ground and one of her sneakers flew into the street. Mecca stomped her face on the ground and Tamika mumbled inaudible words. Shamel saw Tamika on the verge of damn near dying and grabbed Mecca.

"C'mon, Mecca, let's boogie."

Mecca was out of breath, but stopped to look down at Tamika."Bitch, don't ever come near my crib again!" Mecca spat on her and walked off.

"Now, was all that necessary?" Lou asked Mecca after showing her the vision of the fight.

Mecca laughed. "You damn right it was necessary."

Lou shook his head. "You don't have to use that language, Mecca."

Mecca sucked her teeth and replied. "Does it matter? I'm going to hell anyway! I beat that bitch ass," Mecca teased and chuckled. Then she pointed a finger at Lou like a parent or teacher scolding a child. "Plus, I know who you are. I read the Bible and I even read the Qur'an. You the uh . . ." Mecca snapped her fingers. "You're Satan! That's who you are! I figured it out when you said you don't know why God created people who were going to cause bloodshed among each other, and you wanted to prove Him wrong. I read that in those books!"

Lou began to clap his hands. "Hurray for Mecca, she finally got something right! You thought for a second, instead of just reacting!" Lou stopped clapping, then continued, "If you would have figured things out when you had the chance you would have had a better life."

Mecca sucked her teeth. "You make it seem like I was stupid or something."

"No, not stupid. You just made stupid decisions. Listen, Mecca, I've walked the planet since its creation and you're not the worst person I've seen or met. Wow! I've met people like Hitler, Idi Amin, some of the pharaohs of Egypt. Liars like Columbus and others involved in the most treacherous treatment of human beings, the enslavement of your ancestors. All I did was watch."

"What does this have to do with me?" she asked, cutting Lou off from reminiscing.

Lou folded his arms and rubbed his chin."Well, Mecca, for some reason I kind of felt sorry for you, and you were one of the few people who didn't blame me for the things you did. Honestly, I don't know why you did the things you did." Lou shrugged his shoulders. "Things happen that we have no control over. But a job is a job, so let us continue."

Chapter Sixteen

Even in laughter the heart is sorrowful.
Proverbs 14:13

"My appeal looks good. I'll probably get offered a deal instead of going back to trial," Ruby said to Mecca in the visiting room at the Federal Correctional Center for Women in Ohio.

Ruby put on a few pounds since she'd been down. Her face was puffy around the cheeks with the beginning of a double chin forming on her neck. She tried to conceal the weight gain by wearing a large, beige, prison-issued shirt and pants. Her hair was pulled in a tight ponytail, but the wrinkles developing on her forehead and eyes told of Ruby getting stressed and older.

Mecca listened attentively to her, despite the noise in the crowded visiting room. There were kids running around while their parents, mostly black and Hispanic, engaged in sexual acts performed while guards turned their backs. The visiting room smelled like popcorn and cheap perfume.

"Hopefully everything goes good for you," Mecca replied.

"Yeah, this crooked mu'fucka convicted me on some bullshit. They had no evidence against me for no murders except for the Spanish cat because the police was right there, but there were witnesses that seen him come up behind me with a gun. I got an affidavit from one of the witnesses, some lady from Long Island. There's another witness from uptown, a black dude, but he act like who don't wanna help a bitch. I got his address. I'll send it to you to see what you can do!"

Mecca nodded while unintentionally seeing a black inmate getting oral sex from a fat white girl two tables away from where Mecca and Ruby sat. Mecca thought, *People in jail will deal with any person willing to deal with a person behind bars*. The person could be fat, ugly, a whore, an old lady; it didn't matter as long as they had some ties to the outside world. Men and women in prison were the same.

Looking at Ruby saddened Mecca regardless of how many times she came to visit her, which was usually once a month, depending on where

Ruby was located. The Feds usually transfer inmates to different prisons throughout the country so an inmate won't get too familiar with the prison and area around it. Ruby looked powerless, which was something Mecca wasn't used to, nor Ruby. She conducted herself as if she were still running the show on the streets, though, because Mecca made her feel that way even though Mecca ran things and Ruby's name was forgotten.

Mecca made sure Ruby's commissary account stayed above $5,000. Money that Ruby had when she got locked up, she was spending on high-priced lawyers. She currently had three expensive lawyers working on her appeal. The cost was a little over $1 million.

Mecca kept Ruby updated often on what was going on in the streets. She told her about Dawn, and Ruby only replied, "People get what their hand calls for." Mecca spoke of Shamel so much and so highly that Ruby figured it out.

"You feeling Shamel, ain't you?" Mecca blushed. "Yeah, you feeling him," Ruby replied, already knowing the answer.

To Mecca's surprise, Ruby just smiled and said, "He's a good nigga, Mecca. Better than that Tah cat. I don't trust him. You know how niggas from the ville is. The grimiest they come."

Mecca told Ruby about the incident with Tamika.

"You should have cut her face again. What kind of nigga doesn't do anything to somebody who snitched on them? He a sucker-ass nigga! Leave his punk ass!" Ruby said sternly.

"I'm about done with this nigga." Mecca snorted.

After four hours, the visit ended with Mecca promising Ruby that she would see her next month and find the witness who didn't want to cooperate, and Ruby sending her love to Shamel. Before Ruby hugged Mecca she left her with a last piece of advice. Ruby held her face between her palms like Mecca was still a little girl. Mecca felt a little embarrassed but she just listened.

"Leave that clown, Tah. He going to fuck around and be your downfall."

On her flight home, Mecca thought about everything she and Ruby had talked about. Before she got to the airport she called Shamel and told him to pick her up in two hours at JFK. Mecca smiled at the thought of Ruby finally giving her a blessing when it came to Mecca dealing with boys. She had to admit to herself that she was falling in love with Shamel. She didn't have the heart to tell him because she didn't know if he felt the same way. He showed signs that he was in love, but with guys you never know. Some of them just want steady pussy; a chick they could always run to when other chicks front on them. A chick who would do things sexually with them that another chick wouldn't, and Mecca and Shamel's sexual rendezvous had no limits.

When Mecca got to JFK Shamel was there waiting in his Land Cruiser. When she got in the Jeep, Shamel gave her a kiss on the lips and handed her a rose with a card. The card was a Hallmark card with a brown teddy bear on the front that had a red letter "I" on a white T-shirt. When Mecca opened it, the inside said "Love You." Mecca had butterflies in her stomach and she felt the blood rush to her face. She hugged Shamel tightly and replied, "I love you too, Shamel. No lie." She smiled from ear to ear and playfully slapped Shamel on his shoulder.

"You act like I was gone for a long time, surprising me like this."

Shamel drove, looking at the road ahead. "Five minutes away from you is like a lifetime."

Mecca knew right then and there that she had to leave Tah and commit herself to Shamel. During the ride to Brooklyn, Mecca told him about her visit with Ruby. Shamel smiled when she said that Ruby gave her blessing with dealing with him.

"Next time you go see her, I'm going," Shamel said.

"She'll be feeling that," Mecca replied. When Mecca relayed to him what Ruby had said about her appeal and the witness from Harlem, Shamel became angry at the witness and promised Mecca that he was gonna make sure this nigga do the right thing. Even if they had to pay him whatever.

"Matter of fact, we gonna make that a priority," Shamel said, already putting a plan into action. Mecca nodded in agreement.

Two nights later, as Shamel was exiting his Land Cruiser at a weed spot on Pitkin and Miller Avenue, two cars screeched to a halt and eight men jumped out. Shamel didn't have his gun on him this night and he cursed himself for it when he realized the masked men were not cops. Before he could run or try to fight, he felt something heavy and hard hit him on the back of his head, and everything went black.

When he came to, his vision was blurred for a few seconds and his head hurt like hell. When he was able to focus, he saw that the room he was in looked like hell. He could tell he was in an abandoned tenement by the smell of rotted wood mixed with human waste and whatever animals used the place as shelter. The windows were boarded up and the walls were covered with graffiti, chipped paint, and once-plastered holes. The wooden floor that also had holes was littered with syringes, empty crack vials, and garbage. The two men who stood in front of him had the black ski masks still covering their faces. Shamel looked around for the other men who had kidnapped him, but he couldn't see or hear the presence of any other people in the building.

"What's the deal, son, you all right?" one of the masked men chuckled.

"Fuck y'all niggas want? I ain't got no money like that," Shamel said wearily. Both men started laughing.

"And we're Spiderman and Superman, mu'fucka. We know you got money and the bitch you deal with got mad paper. We gonna see how loyal y'all li'l team is," the other masked man barked.

"Leave her outta this, son. How much you want?" Shamel said, angry.

"Damn, kid. That hit a nerve, huh? This nigga must be in love or something, son," one of the men said to the other.

The other one didn't laugh or join in with the other about Shamel loving Mecca. "I thought you ain't have money like that. Soon as we bring the bitch up you ready to peel, huh? Too late, we called her and told her fifty thousand or your ass is out."

The masked man who didn't laugh at the love joke leaned closer to Shamel. "She got a half hour to drop the money off where we told her or you a body, son."

Shamel recognized the voice. He knew if he let him know that he knew who he was he would definitely leave the building in a bag. There was a time and place for everything, especially revenge.

The other masked man took a cigarette out of a pack of Newports he pulled out of his black fatigue pants, and lifted his mask over his mouth, revealing his mouth. Shamel saw the gold teeth the guy had on his bottom teeth. The word 'Born' was engraved on them.

When Mecca received the call she immediately went to her safe she had hidden in an apartment she rented in Bushwick. No one knew about this apartment except her. She rented it just in case she needed to hide out and no one would be able to tell cops or her enemies where she was. The caller told her, "We got Shamel. If you think we lying, go pick his truck up on Pitkin and Miller where we picked him up from. If you want to see him alive, we need fifty thousand. Drop it off in the garbage bin on the corner of New Lots in a half hour." The phone clicked off.

Mecca drove to Pitkin and Miller with one of Shamel's soldiers and tears welled up in her eyes when she saw his truck. She knew something was wrong when he never returned from the weed spot. She told Shamel's soldier to take the truck back to Sutter Gardens and "get ready for war."

Mecca dropped the fifty thousand where she was told, then drove off. Back in the tenement, a third man wearing a mask appeared in the room and whispered in the other masked man's ear. The man whose voice Shamel recognized nodded his head, then bent over, putting his face close to Shamel. Shamel could smell the alcohol on the guy's breath through the wool mask.

"I guess that bitch love you or something 'cause she paid for your freedom and life nigga. Next time, have your heat on you, stupid!"

All the while, Shamel was trying to get his hands loose from the duct tape around his wrist and ankles. His hands were taped behind his back and he was sitting on a crate with his back against the dirty wall. One of the masked men pulled out an orange box cutter and it made a clicking noise as the blade was pushed out.

"Let's see if she'll be attracted to you or pay for your plastic surgery after this."

Shamel started struggling to get his hands loose. He knew what was next. Unfortunately, the tape was too strong and thick for him to break loose. The masked man without the box cutter began punching Shamel in his face and body with fast punches. He felt his eye begin to swell and blood flowed out of his nose. He could taste the blood in his mouth as the guy kept punching.

Fortunately, he was in shape, so the body punches didn't affect him, but the blows to the face were making him dizzy and the pain was excruciating. Then the worst happened.

"Hold his face, son, I'ma eat this nigga food!" the one with the box cutter yelled.

One of them held his face as Shamel tried to turn away. He felt a pinch, then a burning sensation. The masked men then put duct tape around his eyes. They picked him up under his arms and dragged him off the crate, down some stairs, which seemed like they went on forever, banging against his butt and legs.

"Open the door, son!"

The cold night air rushed in as the door opened. Shamel felt the air cooling the blood on his face, which was numb. In the distance, he heard cars driving by and police sirens. Then the men let him go, and his head hit the ground. Lying still, he wondered what the men were doing until he heard them open a car door.

"Cut the tape from his wrist, son!" one of them yelled. Hearing the sound of the box cutter open made his body tense.

"Turn around, mu'fucka!" someone said, tugging on his arm. With the strength he had, Shamel turned over on his side and let the guy cut the duct tape off his wrist. When his hand was freed, he pulled the tape off of his face at the same time he heard a car door slam and tires screeching.

By the time he got the tape off his eyes and pulled it from his ankles, his kidnappers were gone. Shamel looked around the neighborhood to see where he was. The block was filled with tenements; some abandoned, some not. The sidewalk was filled with piles of black industrial garbage bags and littered with garbage, baby diapers, and drug paraphernalia. He touched his face and felt the deep gash and the swelling. He looked at his hands and saw that they were covered in blood.

The block looked familiar; he knew he was in Brooklyn, but was unsure where. He looked at a street sign as the elevated train at the corner rode by, making a screeching sound. Shamel could see the sparks of electricity from under the train as he read the sign: Hull Street and Broadway. He knew he was in Brownsville. Shamel walked to a pay phone on Broadway and dialed Mecca's cell phone. She picked up on the first ring.

"Hello!"

Shamel never felt happier to hear someone's voice. "Mecca, it's me."

"Shamel, where you at?" Mecca screamed into the phone, sounding relieved.

"Come get me. I'm on Hull and Broadway. I know who did this."

"Don't move, I'll be right there. I'm sorry, Shamel," Mecca cried.

"Don't sweat it, Mecca. This ain't your fault. These niggas going to pay. Hurry up, though. Niggas ate my food, I'm leaking."

Chapter Seventeen

Revenge is like the sweetest joy
next to getting pussy.

Tupac

The image of Lou was now dressed in a Catholic archbishop's robe. The yellow and purple robe had gold crosses on the crest and Lou held a large, black Bible in his hands. He opened the Bible and looked at Mecca.

"Mecca, you ever heard the saying 'vengeance is mine saith the Lord'?"

"Yeah, I have been to church before. Damn, I wasn't always in the street," Mecca countered, sounding aggravated.

"I'm not a psychiatrist. I'm not going to ask you why you're so angry even in death, but," Lou said loudly, "you've been angry all your life so you carried it with you to the other side," Lou said, rubbing his palms together. "Now, I asked you about revenge. Don't you think it's rather odd that the creator says revenge is his, but he made it so humans would feel the urge to avenge themselves against their adversaries? Are you following me?"

Mecca looked at Lou confused and shrugged her shoulders.

"I figured you would do that," Lou said. He began to pace back and forth. "It's a catch-22, Mecca. It's not fair, where is the mercy in that? You create something to be able to do as it feels, but you punish them for the choices you gave him. Is that love? No, it's a game!"

"Why are you telling me this? If you have issues with God or whoever, take that up with Him, Her, Them, but leave me alone!" Mecca barked.

Lou put his hand against his heart. "I'm not bothering you, Mecca, I'm trying to teach you something," Lou replied.

"What good does it do me now? What is this knowledge going to do for me? I'm dead."

"Mecca, knowledge is infinite. You never know what will become of you. Who knows what His Greatness has in store for you?" Lou paused and smiled. "I'm just doing my job."

Mecca picked Shamel up in her red Lexus and took him to Kings County Hospital, where he was stitched up. He received a hundred and three stitches for his face, and was released from the hospital the same night.

Shamel's face was numb from the Novocain they used to put the stitches in. He could barely speak when Mecca drove back to East New York. He reclined in the passenger seat with a large gauze pad on the left side of his face. His whole face was swollen, and to anyone who knew him, he was unrecognizable.

"Who did this shit, Shamel? It was Tah, wasn't it?" Mecca asked with the look Shamel had seen on her face when she went after Tamika. It was a look that made her seem like a different person, like when Bruce Banner got angry and was about to transform into the Hulk.

To Mecca's surprise, Shamel shook his head and struggled when he replied, "It was those niggas Kaheem and Born."

"You can't be serious." Mecca's face turned into a look of disbelief.

"Yeah," Shamel replied in a groggy voice.

"Your own cousins? Why the fuck would they . . ." Mecca banged on the steering wheel. "Niggas is real shiesty, Shamel. You treat them niggas like your little brothers. You did everything for them niggas!" Mecca wondered why when she called Kaheem's house, his girl said she ain't see him in a few days. When Mecca told the soldier of

Shamel's who came with her to pick up his truck what happened, he asked when the last time was that anyone had seen Kaheem and Born.

Mecca didn't think anything of it at the time because she was so worried about Shamel. She thought maybe they were at some chick's crib doing whatever. The last thing she would have thought was that they were involved in a kidnapping for ransom on their own cousin. *How grimy is that?* she thought.

The thought if it brought a lump up in Shamel's throat. He fought to hold back the tears. His mind flashed back to when his cousins Kaheem and Born, both twenty years old now, came from Brownsville to stay with Shamel and his grandmother after their house burned down, killing their mother and their little sister, who was two years old.

Kaheem and Born were both fifteen years old when they came to stay with him. A lot of people thought they were twins, but they were really eight months apart. They were both out-of-control teens. They did everything together from crime to sharing women when it came to sex. Both of them did time in juvenile facilities for dozens of robberies around the city. Shamel introduced them to the drug game, thinking that if they made good money it would calm them down and stop them from committing petty robberies.

"It ain't no money in that bullshit chain-snatching, sticking-up-corner shit," Shamel would school them.

He eventually convinced them to join his team and he put them in charge of giving out product to the workers and collecting money. Since he knew they had a sweet tooth for violence, he gave them the positions, so if any of the workers messed up some of the money, Kaheem and Born enjoyed chastising the offender. Sometimes they would go too far and Shamel would have to intervene. When Kaheem and Born found out that Shamel was getting his product from a female, they began to think that Shamel was getting soft.

"Yo, son, Shamel get his work from that chick Mecca," Kaheem said to Born.

"Word? How you know, son?"

"He told me," Kaheem roared.

Born looked astonished. "That pretty-ass chick got work like that?"

"Yeah, and Shamel in love with her. He fucking her and the bitch got a man . . ." Kaheem snapped his fingers and continued. "Matter of fact, she fuck with Tah Gunz from Brownsville Houses. You know she originally from the ville."

"I thought Shamel bust his gat? Fuck he doing working for a chick? She supposed to give everything to him and play her position," Born said.

Kaheem shook his head with a disappointed look on his face. "Shamel got soft on us. I know the nigga fam and he looked out for us, but niggas gonna say we all work for the bitch and think something sweet about us. Something got to give, son."

"So what up, son? Let's do what we do best," Born said with a mischievous grin on his face. Kaheem nodded in agreement with the same grin.

Shamel couldn't believe that his own flesh and blood would do him so dirty, but the situation would definitely be handled. He was thankful that he had a ride or die chick like Mecca by his side, and knew if shit got sticky he could always turn to her for help.

"Don't worry, Shamel, everything gonna be all right," Mecca said, rubbing his thigh. Mecca looked over at Shamel and could see the pain in his eyes. Well, the one eye that was open. The other was swollen shut from the punches he took to the face by his kidnappers.

Shamel looked at Mecca for a few seconds, and then looked out the passenger window. "Word to my grandmother soul, I'm gonna kill them niggas, Mecca."

Mecca put what she had to do for Ruby on hold to tend to Shamel while he healed. She drove over to his building every morning to make him breakfast in bed. She helped him dress and she cleaned his face and changed his gauze pad. To put him more at ease she would suck his dick and let him cum in her mouth. His ribs were sore so she laid him on his back and rode him.

Tah came over to her apartment twice a week and Mecca would treat him like a stranger. When he tried to have sex with her she would turn him down.

"I don't know what that bitch Tamika got. You ain't gonna be fucking me after you fucked her."

Tah would accuse her of fucking Shamel and say that was the reason she didn't want to have sex with him. Mecca would ignore him and Tah would leave. Eventually Mecca started seeing less and less of Tah, except when he collected money from his soldiers and copped coke off Mecca and took the consignment.

Mecca knew eventually Tah was going to be a problem. She figured Tah would eventually feel that if she was no longer his girl, he shouldn't do business with her or look over her other spots in Brownsville, and that's exactly what started to happen.

Mecca got the word that her spots in Langston Hughes and Tilden were constantly being robbed and no one knew who was doing the stick ups.

When Mecca asked Tah about it, he simply said, "I can't be in three places at one time. I'm saying you should put your boy Shamel in charge of those spots. Ain't nobody doing it in my projects. Niggas respect who I be."

When Mecca spoke to Shamel about it, Shamel knew exactly what Mecca knew. "He knows because he's the one who got niggas doing it," Shamel said.

"I ain't been showing my face around the ville. Mu'fucka think that I'm on some high posty shit," Mecca replied.

Shamel shook his head. "Nah, Mecca. Niggas know you a female and even though you bust your guns, niggas still can't grasp the thought of a girl running a spot. Another strike is that you're not out there on the front lines. Niggas respected your aunt so off the strength niggas went with the flow, but how long will you last just off the strength of who your aunt is? You aunt is not here so niggas don't give a fuck no more."

Mecca slammed her fist into her palm. "I'ma show these niggas I ain't no soft-ass chick!"

Shamel grabbed Mecca's hands in his, and then kissed her softly on the lips. "Chill, Mecca, you ain't got to do nothing. That's what I'm here for. I'm going to handle this. You my woman now and I ain't gonna have you running around getting into no shootouts with niggas. I got this."

Three weeks after the kidnapping of Shamel, as the swelling on his face disappeared, Shamel was back out on the streets. The scar on his face was still raw and pinkish, giving Shamel a menacing look. Shamel called Kaheem's girlfriend and Kaheem answered the phone.

"Shamel, what up, son!" he bellowed, sounding as if he were happy to hear from his cousin.

"Ka, what up. Where you been, kid?"

"A yo, son, me and Born was out of town in B-More trying to get something going out there. There's crazy paper out there, son," Kaheem lied.

Shamel kept his cool and talked as if he didn't know that it was his own cousins who kidnapped him and cut his face. "You heard what happened, right?" Shamel asked.

"Yeah, son. We gonna find out who did that foul shit and it's on!" Kaheem said, trying to sound sincere and angry about what happened to Shamel. Shamel could tell that Kaheem covered the phone with his hand. He heard him mumbling in the background.

"Where Born at?" Shamel inquired, setting his plan in motion.

"Still in B-More. He fucks with some bird out there. Nigga act like he in love or something," Kaheem chuckled.

"When he get back in town, y'all come see me, all right?"

"I'm saying if shit is back to normal. I'll be back on the block tonight," Kaheem replied while getting a stronger grip on his girlfriend's hair as she sucked his dick.

"That'll be good. Yeah, come through."

Dear Aunt Ruby,

I hope that by the time you receive this letter you'll be in the best of health physically and mentally. As for me, I'm maintaining and holding things down. A lot of shit has been going on and I feel like I'm going to have to go there. Shamel got kidnapped and niggas cut his face. I had to cough up paper to the cats who got him or Shamel would have made the column. Tah on some other shit. All of a sudden gates in the ville get held up and he dumb to who or what. I know he behind it all because I ain't fucking with him. Times are hard and I need you. Things ran smooth when you were home. Niggas and bitches think I got soft, but I swear I didn't. I'm going to prove to you that I didn't. When you come home, things will still be on the up. Aunt Ruby, write me back ASAP and let me know what you think and what I should do. I miss you and I'm coming up next month.

Love, Mecca

***

When Mecca went to her mailbox a week later, she kind of expected Ruby's response to be short and to the point, but Mecca wished Ruby would at least break things down more. Reading the response, Mecca knew her aunt was angry at her.

Dear Mecca,
Take care of what I asked you to do.
Ruby

Chapter Eighteen

Faithful are the wounds of a friend; but the kisses of an enemy are deceitful.

Proverbs 27:6

"There's a proverb in the Bible, Mecca, that says, 'Hell and destruction are never full: so the eyes of man are never satisfied'," Lou quoted. He continued, "Never satisfied, how true that is," Lou snickered. "Greed, greed, greed. Humans are greedy! How did you put up with conniving, low-down people and still feel that it was worth it?"

"You just don't understand. I had to do what I had to do," Mecca responded with candor.

Lou howled with laughter. "You're wrong, I do understand. I understand that your whole life you've been surrounded by these types of people. Hate to have to say it to you, but your parents were those types of people too."

"I wasn't around them long enough for that," Mecca growled, angry at Lou's comment.

"That's so unfortunate. All I'm saying is that you were raised to think that what you were doing was right, but at some point with all you were going through, you should have realized nothing good would come of that life. Your family was the perfect example of why you should have stopped."

"Stopped and did what?" Mecca yelled.

"Let's see."

Shamel's grandmother returned from her trip down South. Before she could share the news of how good of a time she had, and advise Shamel and Mecca to save up some money, buy land down there, and get away from these treacherous streets, she was concerned about the scar on Shamel's face.

"Baby, what happened? How did you get that? Lord Jesus!"

"I was fixing a light at Mecca's apartment and one of those florescent bulbs broke and cut my face," Shamel lied, with Mecca cosigning his tale.

"You got to be careful. I bought you and your cousins some stuff back," she said, digging in her black leather suitcase. Shamel watched his bowlegged grandmother walk to her suitcase slowly, as if her bones hurt. He figured her arthritis was getting worse. He acknowledged that for her eighty years of living, her dark chocolate skin, though wrinkled a little, made her look twenty years younger.

She still had pretty long hair, now gray, that reached beyond her shoulders when she didn't have it in a bun. She always dressed as if she was going to church: skirts down to her knees, knee-high stockings with shoes that nurses wore, and a blouse buttoned up to the top. Shamel rushed over to help her open the suitcase.

"Thank you, baby. I brought y'all some shirts that are nice. They look as good as those expensive clothes y'all waste y'all money on. Y'all crazy with them ninety-dollar shirts and pants, and hundred-dollar sneakers."

Shamel looked at Mecca, shrugging his shoulders as his grandmother pulled out multicolored, flannel, button-down shirts and some blue and black jeans. The kind they sold in Sears or gave you in prison.

"Ain't they nice?" she asked, holding up a shirt, showing Shamel. "And look at these jeans. They just like the ones y'all wear and I only paid twenty dollars for the shirt and pants together! Clothes are cheaper in the south than up here!

This city is so crazy I got to go, and so should y'all! Mecca, you're a pretty girl. Ain't no pretty girl like you need to be wasting her time in this crazy place. These guys have no respect for women up here. Down south they treat you like a lady, you hear me?"

"Yes, ma'am," Mecca replied.

Shamel's grandmother handed him the clothes. "Go try them on, and give these to those two knucklehead cousins of yours. Those two are up to no good. Where they been? I ain't seen them in a while before I left. Tell them I said don't be calling me from no Rikers Island asking for bail. I'll tell that judge to keep they little tails in there."

Shamel threw the clothing on his bed. "Grandma, I'll try them on later. I got to make a run!" Shamel yelled from his room. He walked out of his room and waved his hand to Mecca, signaling for them to leave.

"Okay, baby. Don't forget to tell those knuckleheads I wanna see 'em."

"I ordered the double cheeseburger, son!"

"Nah, nigga, I did. This your Big Mac!" Kaheem and Born argued in front of a McDonald's on Broadway and Kosciusko Street in Bushwick. Kaheem held the McDonald's bag in his hand while Born tried to reach in and grab the double cheeseburger.

"What difference does it make? Just come on!" Kaheem's Puerto Rican girlfriend yelled while she folded her arms, trying to keep warm from the cold night air. Her cream complexion was red from the frigid wind. The black and red North Face kept her upper body warm but the tight-fitting Parasuco Jeans that gripped her heart-shaped, plump ass didn't protect her from the cold.

"It's cold as hell and you dumb-ass niggas wanna argue over some burgers. Kaheem, let's go!"

Kaheem and Born both looked at her at the same time and in unison barked, "Shut the fuck up!"

"Y'all niggas need to get a life, for real."

"Karmen, you get yourself a job and all of the sudden we gotta get our lives together. You got the nerve to ask Mecca to come work with you at this bullshit McDonald's!" Kaheem grumbled while Born laughed.

"Some people change. Unlike y'all dumb asses y'all want to be in the streets forever. This shit don't last forever, y'all gonna wind up in jail . . ."

Kaheem and Born finished the sentence with Karmen, "Or dead!"

"We heard it all before, Karmen. Come up with something new. Nothing last forever, man," Kaheem said.

Karmen thought Mecca would at least give it a try. She and Mecca became friends when Kaheem brought Karmen to Shamel's crib. They double-dated twice and Karmen and Mecca clicked. Karmen liked Mecca's style. She knew Mecca was real and not like the fake chicks in her neighborhood who smiled in your face and gossiped behind your back.

After Dawn, Mecca told herself she would never get close to another chick like that. In fact, Mecca kept her circle extremely small. Shamel and her aunt. Yet, she could not help but be drawn to Karmen. Karmen talked about a lot of things besides men and materialistic things. Karmen had goals. She wanted to save up money and open a restaurant that served soul food and Spanish food. She wanted to eventually leave New York after opening up a chain of restaurants. She loved to cook. She worked in McDonald's to save up money to go to culinary school to become a chef.

Mecca wondered why somebody like Karmen would be in a relationship with a low-life like Kaheem. She figured there was somebody for everybody. Karmen even suggested that she and

Mecca go into business together. Mecca would agree with her, but she thought that Karmen was just a dreamer and it would never happen. As long as she was with Kaheem, he would do nothing but bring her down. A lot of times, Mecca wanted to tell Karmen about what she thought, but it wasn't her business. Maybe Karmen knew something she didn't.

"Whatever, Kaheem, I'm walking. Y'all can argue over some burgers all night if you want, I don't care," Karmen said, starting to walk up Broadway under the elevated train tracks that the J train ran on.

As the train rode by, Karmen looked back to see if Kaheem and Born were behind her. She sucked her teeth when she noticed them still arguing over the burgers. Karmen heard footsteps behind her when she turned. A man who appeared to be a homeless bum bumped into her.

"Damn, watch where you going," Karmen snapped.

"I'm sorry, ma'am," the man said gravely.

Karmen looked him up and down, studying his dirty, ripped-up jeans, old gray sheepskin that looked like a mangy dog, and some old beat-up New Balances that were caked in dirt. Karmen looked at the man's face. It didn't fit the way he appeared. His face looked clean, when he spoke he showed pearly white teeth, and he was clean-shaven. To her, he appeared to be attractive and no older than twenty-five. As Karmen walked passed him, the man turned around and grabbed her from the back in a bear hug.

"What you doing?" Karmen screamed as a car screeched to a halt and the man, who was too strong for Karmen, lifted her head and walked toward the car.

"Get off me! Kaheem!"

By the time Kaheem and Born heard Karmen scream and they took off running toward her, she was already in the back of a black MPV minivan that screeched off. Kaheem pulled his black .357 Magnum and shot at the vehicle until he emptied his gun. "Karmen!" he screamed, watching the back of the MPV disappear into the cold night.

In Mecca's East New York apartment, Shamel's cellular phone rang while he sat in front of Mecca's fifty-two-inch screen television playing Super Nintendo. He answered after the first ring.

"Yo!"

The voice on the phone answered indistinctly, "She said she'll meet you in Queens."

Chapter Nineteen

Open rebuke is better than secret love.
Proverbs 27:5

"Welcome to the Baisley Park Houses," the orange and blue sign said as you came into the eight-story, brown brick housing project on Guy R. Brewer Boulevard in South Jamaica, Queens. It was a notorious neighborhood that bred one of the most infamous drug gangs in the city of New York; a project that filled the pockets of hustlers with millions. The people of Jamaica, Queens called it "The Baisley."

Shamel had a partner he met on Rikers Island from the Baisley, and he would let Shamel use the apartment to hide out from the police in Brooklyn if needed. He also let Shamel use it when he was creeping on Mecca.

"You think he would put up the money?" Shamel asked Karmen, referring to his cousin putting up ransom money for her.

"If he did that to you, I know he don't give a fuck about me," Karmen said to Shamel as she sat at the kitchen table eating four chicken wings and fried rice off of a Styrofoam plate from the Chinese restaurant. Shamel sat on the other side of the small wooden table eating a pastrami and cheese sub sandwich.

"I told you before, Shamel, he can't be trusted. Neither of them," Karmen continued.

Shamel pulled his cellular phone out of his black and red Avirex leather jacket and set it on the table in front of Karmen. "Call him and find out. You got to put the act on. You know, sound like you're scared and all that."

"C'mon, Shamel, you know I know how to act. I got this, watch the performance." Karmen smiled and grabbed the phone. Karmen dialed Kaheem's cellular phone, and he answered on the first ring.

"Who this?"

"Kaheem, come get me, boo, they gonna kill me!" Karmen said in a shaky and terrified tone. She hoped she sounded believable over the phone.

"Karmen, you all right, ma?" Kaheem asked, sounding concerned.

"Yeah, Papi, I'm fine, but they want thirty G's and they'll let me go!"

"Karmen, listen. You know where you at?"

"No. Just come—"

Shamel grabbed the phone and disguised his voice the way Kaheem and Born tried to do when they kidnapped him.

"A yo, duke, thirty G's. Drop it off on Linden Boulevard by the weed spot. Right on the block where the car lot is at. You got an hour."

Before Shamel hung up he heard Kaheem say, "A yo, hold up, son. Listen. That bitch ain't worth nothing to me. Do what you gonna do."

Shamel let Karmen listen to what Kaheem said by putting the phone between his ear and hers. Karmen was hurt by what he said, but not shocked. She shrugged her shoulders,

"Oh, well, we knew what to expect though," Karmen said, getting up and throwing the plate of Chinese food in the garbage.

"Damn, niggas ain't shit!" Shamel grumbled.

"You should know that. You ain't shit either, or is this pussy so good you can't turn it down?" Karmen said as she sat on Shamel's lap and ran a finger along Shamel's ear. He grabbed her ass and squeezed through the jeans, grinning.

"You want me to answer that?" Shamel spoke as he smiled in her face. Karmen grabbed Shamel's crotch and felt his hard dick under his pants.

"Damn, that big boy ready, huh? To answer your question, I want you to answer mines by fucking this pussy."

Karmen stood up and unzipped her jeans, pulling one pant leg down, exposing the red lace thong she had on underneath. At the same time Shamel pulled his pants down to his ankles, letting his dick poke out through the hole in his blue silk boxers. Karmen pulled her thong to the side and sat on his stiff dick.

"Ay, Papi, I know Mecca's pussy ain't better than this."

"I can't get involved in that. Those cops are going to harass me."

"So you're just going to allow a woman who was protecting herself from a man trying to kill her to sit in jail for life?" Mecca asked the eyewitness from Harlem who saw the Spanish man creeping up on Ruby try to shoot her.

Mecca was dressed in an ocean green blazer with a white blouse underneath and a beige skirt that made her look like she was a businesswoman. Her hair was neatly pressed out to her shoulders, with a part running down the middle of her head. The witness looked like a nerdy computer wiz who lived alone, sitting at his computer all day, drinking tea and eating potato chips. He was a brown-skinned, frail-framed, twenty-five- year-old college student from Rhode Island attending Columbia University. He tried to close the door of the brownstone on 138th and Morningside, but Mecca jammed her foot between the door and the frame.

"Please just leave me alone. I'll call the police!"

Mecca sighed and put on a sad demeanor. "Please, man, she's my aunt, and she's all I have. Just please help her."

"I don't think I can help her anyway. From what I hear, she's in jail for other murders. She's not an innocent person I just seen protecting herself, she's a monster," the guy said, watching Mecca's facial expression change from a pleading one to a face of fury and rage. Mecca stared at him coldly for a few seconds, moved her foot, and let him close the door. Then she walked away.

The witness looked through the glass on the wooden door at Mecca's back and shook his head. "People are crazy these days."

If the man knew who Mecca was, he would have taken the $100,000 she had offered him and signed the affidavit. If he knew what that look in Mecca's face meant, he would have packed up and headed back to Rhode Island. Instead, he put it all behind him and forgot all about Ruby and that day. The witness remembered the look on Ruby's face when she emptied her gun. It was the same look he just saw on Mecca's face.

Later that night, the police dispatcher at the thirty fourth precinct received a call that a black male was found dead on a Harlem sidewalk, apparently from jumping off the roof, committing suicide. The caller told the dispatcher that it happened on 138th and Morningside.

Lou closed his eyes and shook his head. Mecca wanted to scream, but she didn't. She would have never guessed that Shamel would cheat on her. Especially with Karmen, a girl that Mecca had grown to like. A girl she considered a friend. Shamel, the man she would have died for. A man whose ransom she didn't hesitate to pay to his own cousins. A man she loved with all her heart and left her man for.

"Let me ask you something, Mecca. If you knew or found out all this before you were shot, what would you have done with your life?"

"I don't know," Mecca answered in a low tone with her head down.

"I know. You would have killed them all. Wouldn't you?" Lou yelled.

Mecca simply shook her head. "I don't know!"

"There's no doubt in my mind you would have killed them all. Still in all, Karmen did offer to help you change your life. It's the least she could do even though she was having sex with your man," Lou grinned, then continued, "So sinister are you humans, but, Mecca, there's a lot more I have to show you. The worst is yet to come."

"How much worse could it get?" Mecca looked at him, astonished.

"Beyond your wildest imagination. Shall we proceed?"

Chapter Twenty

It is better to dwell in the corner of the housetop, than with a brawling woman and in a wide house.
Proverbs 24:24

Karmen limped into her Bushwick apartment looking as if she had been raped and beat up. Her nose had dried blood on it, her hair was tossed, and her red and black North Face was ripped after Shamel promised to buy her new clothes.

"C'mon, Papi, why we gotta rip the North Face? I already let you punch me in the face. I like that coat."

"As soon as we do what we gotta do, I'm going to take you shopping, all right?" Shamel promised, pinching her cheek playfully and kissing her on the lips.

"You promise?" Karmen asked in a childish tone.

Shamel held up his left hand as if he were taking an oath in court. "I swear on everything I love."

Karmen limped into her bedroom where she found Kaheem sleeping. She turned the light on, brightening up the small tenement room with pink painted walls with posters of Nas, Mary J. Blige, and Fat Joe and his Terror Squad crew. She had pictures taped to the wall of her and her friends at the Puerto Rican Day parade, and a framed picture of her and Kaheem on the nightstand next to a digital clock radio beside the small bed. A nineteen-inch television sat on top of a small wooden shelf in the corner of the room next to a four-wheel shopping cart filled with clothes she washed at the Laundromat.

Kaheem woke up when the light came on. Wiping the cold out of his eyes with both hands, he said in a groggy voice, "Hey, what's up, ma, you all right?"

Karmen took off her coat slowly as if she were in pain and rolled her eyes at Kaheem getting out of the bed. "Does it look like I'm all right? And what the fuck you doing in my house, you wasn't going to help me come home. Those mu'fuckas was going to kill me."

Kaheem walked toward Karmen and tried to hug her. Karmen pushed him away from her.

"Kaheem, get the fuck away from me. You ain't shit."

"Listen, ma, I knew if I acted like I didn't care they would let you go. They wouldn't have gained nothing by killing you." Kaheem tapped his temple with his index fingers grinning. "It was all part of my plan."

"So you gonna play games with my life? You rather risk me getting raped or killed than pay twenty or thirty G's. Money you have, mu'fucka? If you loved me, you would have done the same thing Mecca did!"

"How you think I know how to play this, Karmen?" Kaheem said. He stepped closer to her and whispered like someone else was in the house. "I wouldn't have killed my cousin. I knew Mecca would have paid though."

Karmen acted as if she were shocked to hear what Kaheem said. "You did that shit, Ka?" Karmen asked loudly.

Kaheem put his finger to his lip. "Shhh, Karmen. Damn, don't let the whole Bushwick hear you. Yeah, I did it. Me and Born."

"Why you had to cut his face, though, Ka? That's your cousin!"

"Man, fuck that nigga. He don't give a fuck about me and Born, all he care about is himself and Mecca. He lucky we ain't body his ass. The nigga got soft anyway. He washed up."

Kaheem heard the squeak of the bedroom door being opened, and before he could grab his pants to get his gun, Shamel already had his silver and gray .40-caliber automatic pistol with a red beam pointed at Kaheem's forehead. Shamel had tears in his eyes.

"All the shit I did for you niggas and it's fuck me, Ka? That's how it is?"

Kaheem held up protesting hands. "Son, it don't gotta be this way, for real!"

Shamel moved closer. "What way it gotta be then?" He looked at Karmen and spoke, "Karmen, go downstairs and wait for me."

Kaheem looked at her and Shamel, confused. Karmen did as she was told, angering him even more.

"Karmen, where the fuck you going? Stay your ass right here. He ain't your man!"

Karmen kept walking and shot back, "You ain't my man neither."

"Yo, Karmen! Fuck you, bitch."

Kaheem went to reach for his pants. "Son, don't move, 'cause the next time you do, I'ma squeeze," Shamel said, kicking Kaheem's pants away from him. Shamel felt the gun in it as he did.

"Why you snake me like that, Ka? I ain't been nothing but good to y'all niggas. If you needed some paper you could have asked me. You ain't have to do this. Then you gonna eat my food," Shamel said quietly.

Kaheem thought about why he envied his older cousin. He wasn't attractive as Shamel was, but he wasn't an ugly dude. He was a slim, brown-skinned, tall dude who favored Marlon Wayans. Shamel got all of the pretty chicks, while Kaheem and Born got the average hood rats. He always had more money than them and Kaheem was tired of being looked at as Shamel's little cousin. He wanted his own identity. Because Kaheem and Born were born eight months apart, Born being the youngest, they resembled each other. Born was just shorter and darker, traits he got from his mother, while Kaheem favored their father.

Trying to sound as if he wasn't scared, Kaheem asked, "So you gonna kill me, Sha? I'll give you the money back, son. I just needed a quick buck and I figured Mecca would cough it up."

"So why you pick me for bait?" Shamel yelled.

Kaheem stood with his hands to his side. "Who else, son? Mecca don't give a fuck about nobody. Not Tah Gunz or nobody except you and her aunt. Her aunt ain't here so it's you."

"Nigga, we supposed to be family!" Shamel said with tears rolling down his face.

"I'm saying, son, I fucked up. I'm sorry, kid. What else can I say?" Kaheem pleaded.

"Nothing."

Shamel squeezed the trigger and the first bullet hit Kaheem in the stomach, making him bend over forward. The second bullet caught him on the top of his head, shattering his skull and sending blood and brains out, landing on Karmen's bed.

Karmen sat in Shamel's blue and silver Grand Am looking up at the window of her third-floor apartment. She watched as Shamel removed the sheet she used for curtains and lifted the window. Shamel looked out and then ducked his head back in, emerging with a black plastic garbage bag. He threw the bag on the fire escape, then climbed out. He leaned on the rail looking up and down the block to see if anyone was coming. The street was empty.

Karmen could see the smoke from the cold air coming out of Shamel's mouth fast. Shamel lifted the bag and threw it on a pile of garbage bags on the sidewalk in front of the building.

Karmen waited another fifteen minutes, and then Shamel came out the front door carrying her sheets and blanket. He walked over to the car and told Karmen to roll down the window.

"Hold these. I'll be back," Shamel said in a low tone.

Karmen grabbed the blanket and sheets then quickly rolled the window back up. She threw them on the backseat, then watched Shamel drag the garbage bag into the alley on the side of her building.

He went so far into the alley that the dark night engulfed him and Karmen could not see him. A few seconds later, he emerged and skipped over to the driver's side and got in. He pulled a cassette tape out of his glove compartment and put it in the tape player. He started the car up and sped off just as the Notorious B.I.G.'s voice barked, "Who shot ya?"

Shamel dropped Karmen off at Mecca's apartment and told Mecca he'd be back. Born was coming to see Shamel and his grandmother. Mecca was more than happy to let Karmen stay with her after Shamel told her what happened.

"Let her lay low here for a few days, then she can go back home."

Before Shamel left, Mecca asked him if he was going to take the trip with her that weekend to see Ruby. Shamel touched his scar and said, "I ain't ready to go see her yet. Not while I'm still a little bruised. Tell her I send my love and I'm definitely coming next month."

Mecca understood how he felt. She wouldn't have wanted to see somebody she hadn't seen in years with brand new wounds on his face, so she didn't press the issue. Shamel had a lot on his plate right now dealing with the betrayal from his own blood, and already killing one and preparing to kill the other. It was a pill Mecca found hard to swallow.

Shamel sat at the oval-shaped, black wooden table with his grandmother, with a plate of smoked turkey, rice, and garlic bread, waiting for Born to join them.

"Where them boys at? Didn't you tell them what I said?" Shamel's grandmother asked, setting two plates on the table for Kaheem and Born.

"I spoke to Brian (Borns birth name), but Kaheem I ain't hear from," Shamel lied.

"They so hardheaded, those two," his grandmother said, frustrated.

Just then, Shamel heard keys and the door opened with Born walking in.

He had on a Coogie sweater with red being the most outstanding color among the other colors that lined it. His Pelle Pelle jeans were pitch black and his suede Wallabee Clarks were died red. A red bandanna hung out of his back pocket.

Shamel shook his head. Shamel knew Born used to be a Five Percenter, but since this Blood thing came to New York, a lot of Five Percenters turned Blood, and Born jumped on the bandwagon. It angered Shamel that Born didn't at least put the bandanna away in the presence of their grandmother, but like his grandmother said, "Them boys are truly knuckleheads."

"Hey, Grandma. When you get back?" Born greeted his grandmother. He hugged her, then sat at the table and gave Shamel a low-toned, "What up, kid?"

Shamel looked at him while chewing his food and simply nodded his head.

Grandma tapped Born on his shoulder, "Go wash your hands, boy! What I tell you about that?" Born jumped up and bopped to the bathroom; all the while, Shamel watched him menacingly.

"What's gotten into you, Shamel?" Grandma asked, seeing the angry look on his face. Shamel forced a smile.

"Nothing, Grandma. I was just wondering why Kaheem ain't here."

"You boys like running the streets like it's something good out here. Ain't nothing but trouble out there and as long as you're out there . . ."

Shamel heard his grandmother talking but his mind was elsewhere. He watched as Born walked back to the table and sat down to start eating. Grandma slapped his hand.

"Boy, say your grace! If you and your brother would have come at the same time, we could have all said grace together for the love of Jesus. You two need the Lord. All y'all need the Lord."

Born acted as if he were praying, then said, "Amen." He knew not to argue with his grandmother about him not believing in a "Mystery God" or a "Spook." He knew he had no wins with her so he just went along with what she said.

"Where's your brother, Brian?"

"I don't know, he probably out looking for Karmen. She disappeared," Born said, looking down at his food.

"Shoot. She probably tired of his crap. He ain't got no job and he lay around on his tail all day. A woman ain't going to constantly put up with no lazy man. A real woman at least," Grandma commented.

After they ate the meal with pound cake for dessert, Grandma cleaned off the table and went in the kitchen to wash the dishes. Born took out a cigarette from a pack of Newports he had in his pocket. He was about to light it when Shamel said, "Don't do that, you know she ain't with that smoking in here, and neither am I."

Born put it down and looked at Shamel curiously. "What's up with you, son? You act like you ain't got no holla for a nigga. Ice grillin' me all night. I ain't the nigga who did you wrong. I'm family, kid." Born smiled.

Shamel chuckled, "Family, huh?"

Born stood up. "Grandma, I'll be back."

"Where you going now?" Grandma yelled.

Born walked to the door with Shamel in tow. "I'm going out to smoke a cigarette."

"Okay, baby!"

Shamel and Born went in front of the building and stood in the foyer, and Born smoked his cigarette while leaning against the building mailboxes.

"Sha, what's up, son? You chillin'?"

Shamel looked out the glass door entrance and exit of the building at passing cars and his Land Cruiser parked in front. Shamel blew into his hands, warming them. He had on a dark blue Polo knitted sweater, a blue Yankee fitted cap that was oversized and hung down almost over his eyes, black Polo jeans, and black leather-six-inch Timberlands.

"I'm chilling, kid. Trying to get this paper."

Born blew out smoke from his mouth, nodding his head. "I hear that, son. Wassup with Mecca? I ain't seen her in a while."

Shamel looked at him out of the corner of his eye. "She chilling. Same shit. Yo, Born, let's take a ride to the weed spot real quick. I got a fifty bag."

Shamel knew Born wouldn't turn a free smoke down. He was a serious weed fiend. He smoked so much he would make Snoop Dogg, Red Man, and Method Man say, "Dayum!"

Born hopped off the mailboxes and followed Shamel to his Land Cruiser. Born was surprised when Shamel drove to the same weed spot he got kidnapped in front of on Pitkin and Miller Avenue. Quickly, he restrained his surprise on his face and looked out the passenger window.

As Shamel pulled up, Born kept his eye on the street, avoiding eye contact with Shamel. Born saw a person standing in front of an alley beside the weed spot disguised as a grocery store. The person had long dreadlocks down to his shoulders. Some of the locks covered the face of the brown-skinned short person wearing a camouflage jacket and pants, with his hand in one pocket.

"Born, duke got that smoke right there. Police raided the spot the other day," Shamel said, handing Born a fifty-dollar bill. Born grabbed the money and stepped out of the Jeep. He dug in his pocket and switched Shamel's fifty-dollar bill for a counterfeit fifty dollar bill he had.

"Dread, gimme fifty," Born said, holding the money out.

In a Jamaican accent, the dread asked, "You wan' chocolate or you wan' skunk, my yoot?"

Born tried to look in the dread's face who had his head down, looking in a sandwich bag that contained small plastic bags with weed in it. He thought the dread sounded as if he were trying to hide his real voice. When he asked Born what he wanted, it sounded like a female trying to deepen her voice. Born ignored the thought, thinking it's probably him tripping off the dust he smoked before he showed up at his grandmother's house for dinner.

"Let me get that chocolate," Born replied.

For a split second, Born took his eyes off the dread to look up and down the block for cops or an enemy. It was in that split second that he felt something slam into his temple after hearing a loud bang in his ears. Then everything went blank.

The dread stood over Born's body with a .357 Magnum Blue steel in his hand now pointed down at Born. The dread put five more bullets into his body before running off and jumping into a candy-apple red Lexus parked a few spaces behind where Shamel parked his Jeep. When Mecca jumped in her Lexus, she removed the wig and followed Shamel's Jeep happy, that everything went as planned.

Chapter Twenty-one

". . . stay civilised, time flies/ incarcerated,
your mind dies.

Nas

"Maybe you need to wear a suit more often," Mecca said to Shamel, who was dressed in a black double-breasted Italian silk suit. He smirked at her, watching the reflection in the full-length mirror in front of him.

"The only time you'll see me in a suit is at times like this."

"That was a good deal they gave us for a double funeral," Mecca commented.

Shamel's grandmother wanted funeral services for her two grandsons together. When she received the call about Kaheem, she didn't cry. She had mentally prepared herself for that call when they first came to live with her. Then the call came about Born, which caught her by surprise because they both got murdered a few hours apart from each other, but not together. She did eventually shed a few tears for her grandsons and prayed.

"Lord, I know those children were always up to no good, and some hardheaded ones, too. But I beg you, Lord, to forgive them and have mercy on their souls."

Mecca wore a black Chanel dress that reached her knees and hugged her curves. She complimented her dress with two-karat, princess-cut diamond earrings and a black Chanel pocketbook. Her black four-inch heels were by Gucci.

The men who attended the funeral, who were mostly friends of Kaheem and Born, simply stared at her as if she were the star of the show. The women, who were either girlfriends of the men in attendance or of the many girlfriends Kaheem and Born had, gave Mecca the evil eye. As a show of respect and honor to Kaheem and Born, the men who were their friends and associates showed up in red suits, and some wore red street clothing with bandannas around their wrists.

The funeral was held in a funeral home called Unity in Brownsville. Shamel, his grandmother, and Mecca sat in front while the others sat behind them in the wooden pews sectioned in two rows. The bodies of Kaheem and Born, dressed in black tuxedos, lay in two cherry wood caskets in front of the mourners. The mortician did a great job at covering up the scars and gunshot wounds on both bodies, and although it wasn't possible to piece Kaheem's skull back together, it was barely noticeable that the top of his head was sewn shut.

A preacher gave a speech about life and death and spoke a few good words about Kaheem and Born, which Mecca knew were lies. To her, there was nothing good about the two scoundrels. All they did was rob and shoot people and snake those close to them. Mecca looked at their bodies and thought, *There lie two no good niggas. The world is better off without them. They deserve to be wherever they are. See you in hell mu'fuckas.*

Mecca turned to look around the funeral home, wondering if someone heard her thoughts, and looked at some of the people, wondering how many of them felt the same way. She smiled at Karmen sitting behind her in a black, button-down, cotton Gap shirt, black Gap jeans, and a pair of black leather Timberland boots.

Karmen half smiled back at her, and she noticed the smile leave Mecca's face as she caught Tah and his crew come inside the funeral home. Tah and his crew entered all dressed in black. The four of them wore black butter soft leathers, baggy jeans, and Timberland chukkas.

Tah looked at Mecca, smiled, and nodded his head as he and his crew found seats in the back. She wondered what Tah was doing there. Did he know Born and Kaheem? Born and Kaheem were from Brownsville, but she didn't think they knew or even associated with Tah. If they did, then could it be that Tah was the mastermind behind Shamel's kidnapping? Mecca was willing to bet he was. How she would find out was another question she needed an answer to, and knew it would be hard to get.

The N.Y.P.D. set up shop outside of the funeral home. Some were on the roof of the building and across the street in marked and unmarked vehicles. They were investigating the murders and wanted to know who Kaheem and Born associated with. It was obvious to them that the two were Bloods, which to the N.Y.P.D. meant anybody could have killed these two.

"Mecca a grimy bitch, son. She know damn well her and duke did this shit and they gonna sit up there acting like they hurt. I like her style," one of the members of Tah's crew whispered in his ear.

Tah smiled and whispered back, "She ain't shit, right?"

Tah hated the fact that Mecca left him for Shamel. Not so much because he loved her, but his ego and pride couldn't deal with some nigga taking something from him. He didn't want people to look at him like he couldn't keep a girl and he had no control, or like she played him. He swore to himself that both of them would pay for their violation.

After the preacher finished his sermon and asked if anyone wanted to say something about the two men (and no one could or would say good things about them), everyone viewed the bodies. The Bloods left red bandannas, bullets, and weed in the caskets and threw gang signs as they passed by the bodies.

Tah and his crew were the first to walk out of the funeral home. They stood around out front hugging people they knew, and staring menacingly at guys they had beefs with in the past or guys they robbed. Tah hugged a girl he knew from Brownsville and his jacket lifted up as he did, revealing the black 9 mm Berretta he had tucked under his belt. A plainclothes cop noticed the gun and immediately spoke into his walkie-talkie.

"I see a gun. I'm going to walk toward the guy. When I get to him, back me up." The cop got out of his unmarked car directly across the street where Tah stood. He walked over to Tah from behind.

"Excuse me. Can I have a word with you?" the cop said, tapping Tah on his shoulder. Tah turned around and looked the white man up and down, curiously.

"Who the fuck is—" Before Tah could finish the sentence, he heard yells from a dozen cops.

"Freeze! Don't move!"

The cop in front of him showed his badge and grabbed Tah by the arm and patted him down. Tah's crew all began walking away as the other cops told the crowd to either walk away or go back into the funeral home. The guys dressed in red all walked away quickly. Some of them also had guns on them. The cop who approached Tah pulled the gun from his pants.

"What you got this for, buddy? Plan on shooting up the funeral?"

Tah grinned as he was cuffed. "Nah."

The cop searched his pockets while another took his arm. "You got anything in your pocket that will stick me? Did you come here to shoot these guys again?"

"Fuck you talking about?" Tah wiped the grin off of his face, puzzled by the officer's comment.

"The dead guys, you come to shoot them again?" The cop continued smiling at Tah.

"Fuck outta here, I ain't shoot nobody!"

The cop walked Tah to one of the marked police vehicles. "Yeah, right, wise ass. You're innocent, huh?"

***

"Did you ever think about taking up acting instead of selling drugs, Mecca?" Lou asked sarcastically after showing Mecca the funeral of Kaheem and Born. "'Cause you're good, you got Halle Berry beat for an Oscar!"

Mecca ignored Lou and thought about what he said. Everyone around her was an actor. Shamel acted as if he truly loved her. So did Tah. Karmen acted as if she was her friend, yet she was fucking Shamel and smiling in her face. *Who else was acting?* she asked herself. Mecca admitted she acted like she didn't kill Born and Kaheem, but they deserved it, and the only reason she had to act that way was to avoid suspicion. She didn't act like that with the people she loved. She was real and loyal to those who were supposed to be her friends and loved ones.

"You're like the jackal," Lou said excitedly. "You disguise yourself and everything. You're amazing!"

Mecca sucked her teeth, but kept silent. She was tired of Lou's antics and this game he was playing with her. She wanted it to end. If she knew that death was like this, and because you did wrong you would have to watch what you did and what others who were supposed to be your friends did, she would have changed her life. But death is the most unsolved mystery that exists.

"But Shamel, he's way better than Denzel Washington. Y'all were made for each other!" He chuckled. "I got to give it to Ruby, though, she is the best who ever did it. No one can compare to the diva, Ruby! That's right, I said it, Ruby is a diva!"

"My aunt is straight up real," Mecca said sternly.

"You ever read in the Bible—"

"Fuck the Bible; I don't wanna hear that shit. Just get this shit over with!" Mecca yelled, cutting Lou off. Lou smiled and bowed as if he finished performing on stage.

Chapter Twenty-two

Federal Courthouse, Brooklyn, 1999

"Objection! Your honor, counsel is retrying the case. This is an evidentiary hearing."

"Counsel, what is your point?"

"Your Honor, with all due respect, I'm trying to show how my client was prejudiced by trial counsel's failure to call these witnesses. These witnesses would have provided that my client was defending herself!"

Ruby sat next to her lawyer dressed in a beige prison suit with her hair cut in a low Afro. She smiled hearing her lawyer argue the case. Mecca and Shamel sat in the spectators' seats, two rows behind the defense table where Ruby and two lawyers sat. Shamel and Mecca were the only spectators in the courtroom, along with court officers, who were standing at the entrance to the courtroom.

"I'm going to overrule the objection. Proceed."

After the two-hour hearing, Mecca spoke with Ruby's attorneys about Ruby's chance of getting a new trial or having the conviction vacated. Mecca dressed in a Dolce & Gabbana powder blue, button-down blouse, and butt-hugging, black khaki pants, with a pair of powder blue Gucci shoes. She held her black Coach bag under her armpit while listening attentively to Ruby's lawyer explain how Ruby's chances looked good, but the courts were unpredictable. The attorney promised to keep Mecca updated on the case; until then they would have to wait.

While Mecca spoke to the attorney, Shamel sat speaking to a shackled Ruby. The judge allowed an in-court visit. She looked Shamel up and down, smiling.

"I knew you were going to be a looker, but damn, I didn't think you would be this fine."

"Stop fronting like you into men again," Shamel joked. Ruby could see that Shamel kept himself in good shape. His frame filled in the gold and black Versace shirt, and Ruby felt a tingle in her pussy.

"When you gonna come visit me again? You in love now, huh? So I can't get no more of that?"

"You know since this shit happened, Mecca hardly lets me out of her sight," he said in a low tone, fingering the scar on his face.

Shamel remembered the last time he snuck off to visit Ruby. She paid the guard to let her sneak off into a bathroom in the visiting room that the staff used. When Shamel walked in, Ruby had her beige prison skirt lifted up to her waist, and was holding on to the sink, bent over.

"Hurry up, Shamel, we got ten minutes."

Shamel quickly pulled his Fila velour pants down and already erect, grabbed his dick and pushed it into Ruby's hairy pussy. Ruby felt Shamel's large dick fill her insides. She thought she felt him in her stomach when he rammed his pole in and out of her. She held her head down and tried to hold her moan in. She inhaled and exhaled loudly.

"Shamel, fuck me ! Fuck me harder!"

After about fifteen minutes, the guard knocked on the door and told Ruby her time was up. The shift was about to change. She fixed herself up before walking out of the bathroom and back to her seat. Shamel walked out a minute later and took his seat at the visitor's side of the table. He knew that dick was Ruby's weakness and he had no quarrels exploiting that fact. He knew if he gave her what he wanted he would get what he wanted. When he wanted her to give Mecca her blessing to mess with him, he gave her one of the best half hours of fucking she ever had on one of their secret visits.

When Ruby was on the streets, he would fuck her when she wanted to go heterosexual for a minute. Then she would reward him with cocaine for him to sell. It was on one of their creeping moments when Shamel suggested to Ruby that she put him in charge of Sutter Gardens by giving him five kilos on consignment and he would re-up from her.When she got locked up he promised Ruby that he would continue to re-up from Mecca and protect her. Ruby agreed.

"She's all I have, Shamel. I went through a lot to get where I'm at and I want to return to the streets the same way I left them!"

Mecca returned to the courtroom, where Shamel was speaking to Ruby. She sat next to Shamel and smiled at her aunt.

"The lawyers said it looks good," Mecca said, enthused.

Ruby shrugged her shoulders. "They been saying that for the last ten years, Mecca. They say whatever to keep that money coming in."

"You know it takes time when it comes to these appeals. You got all them other bodies thrown out. All you got now is this one," Shamel said, trying to lighten the mood. He knew Mecca was in a good mood after speaking to the lawyer. Ruby's attitude toward her possibly having the murder of the Spanish man overturned made Mecca's change.

He didn't want to be around her when she was in a bad mood. He already had to put up with her when she was on her period. Those were the worst three-to-five days to be in her presence. It was on those days that Mecca never second-guessed shooting or cutting somebody. When the marshals told Ruby her in-court visit was over, Ruby gave Mecca and Shamel a warning before they left the courthouse.

"Y'all be easy out there. Stay off them phones and hang them cron's up for a minute. They are looking to that witness who got hit uptown. They trying to link it to me."

When the marshal walked Ruby out of the courtroom, she smiled at Mecca, and without a sound coming out of her mouth, Mecca read "I love you" on Ruby's lips.

Mecca did the same. "I love you too."

When the visit was over, Ruby would return to her cell and cry herself to sleep. She hated the fact that her weakness was a man's penis, dating all the way back to when she was in love with Wise. She despised the fact that a man could control her if he made her orgasm. Her attempt to control her life was one of the reasons she turned to women for sexual gratification. She had no weakness for women.

Before she fell asleep, she got up from the bottom bunk and tapped her cellmate's leg. Her cellmate was a young, black woman who resembled Monique; same complexion, height, and build.

"Kima, I need some attention, baby," Ruby said in a commanding tone.

Kima rolled her eyes and put down a book called *Shattered Souls* written by Dywane Birch. She jumped off the top bunk. Ruby covered the cell door with a sheet then she pulled off her beige prison dress. She laid on her bunk after taking her white panties off. Kima put her knees on the floor and leaned between Ruby's legs and sucked and licked Ruby's pussy. Ruby held her head and closed her eyes and moaned.

"Lick this pussy, Kima."

Tah was back on the streets, and like most cats who returned from prison without plans of going straight, Tah had plans to take over Brownsville regardless of whose toes he stepped on. While he was up north, he got the word that all members of his crew were Bloods and that Brownsville Houses were being run by a Blood cat from East New York. The blood was getting his product from Shamel.

Tah blamed Mecca for everything that happened. Shamel was her boyfriend and he got his product from her. Tah found out that Mecca made Ruby's villa her permanent residence and transformed her East New York apartment into a weed spot. She was selling weed and crack. Word on the street was that Mecca's re-up was fifteen bricks and ten pounds of weed a week.

While Tah was up north, he became a Blood. He moved up in ranks quickly off his rep on the streets and while he was locked up he caught cuttings and stabbings that made him feared throughout the state system. It was the reason he served his whole sentence. By the time Tah served his sentence, he was a general. The word was sent to Brownsville that when Tah came home, he was the general over the ville, and anyone who didn't abide by that would be dealt with accordingly.

"I'm feeling this CLK right here." Tah grinned as he stared at a 1999 candy-apple red CLK 600 Benz.

"It's yours if you want it, son," replied Mo Blood.

He was the Blood from East New York who Shamel put in charge over Brownsville Houses. Mo Blood received the word from his higher-ups in state prison throughout the state that when

Tah returned, he was under his command. Mo Blood was loyal to the U.B.N. (United Blood Nation) and had no quarrels with the order. In fact, he bought Tah a full wardrobe of all the latest fashion, and now they stood in a Benz dealership in Freeport, Long Island so Tah could have a ride.

Tah was feeling good dressed in a red and white Sean John button-down shirt, black Iceberg jeans, and red dolomite Gore-Tex boots, driving his CLK straight off the lot as Mo Blood followed in a silver Range Rover 4.6 with chrome, twenty-inch Sprewell rims. Tah threw in Jay-Z's *Vol.2 Hard Knock Life CD* and drove down the Long Island Expressway, blasting the track where Foxy Brown and Jay spit, "Gotta get that paper dog!" Tah was ready to handle business and was planning to disrupt the entire operation. People had to pay for the time he spent locked up and the money he lost while being away, and at the top of his list were Mecca and Shamel.

Chapter Twenty-three

Wrath is cruel, and anger is outrageous; but who is able to stand before envy?
Proverbs 27:4

Lou stood in front of a bright light. A light too bright for human eyes. A voice spoke from the light as Lou kneeled down.

"Where do you come from?"

"Your Majesty, I come from walking up and down the earth, observing the bloodshed and destruction that humans cause among each other," Lou replied.

"What about the girl?" the voice asked. Lou paused for a few seconds before responding.

"Her ways, her lifestyle, and the people around her are a perfect example of what I've told you from the beginning. These beings you've created above us are unworthy of the praise you give them. With all due respect, Your Majesty, they are weak. I'm trying to understand their psyche. I'm trying to come to terms with why you believe that these animals would love you as I do, most glorified and exalted."

"This is why I cast you and those like you out. You question things; you have no authority to question me. I know what you know not. You're using this child Mecca as a guinea pig for your silly games. You don't understand humans. You walked the earth for millions of years and still can't understand them. It wasn't meant for you to do!"

"I'm not playing a game with her at all, Your Majesty. I actually pity her. Her life has been filled with turmoil and betrayal by those she loves. I can relate to her plight, Your Majesty. This is one I ask for you to show mercy on."

"Continue. What I have planned for her will manifest through her will!"

The image of Lou returned in the eyesight of Mecca.

"What, you took a lunch break or something?" Mecca asked sarcastically.

"Mecca. I'll ask this question again. What would you do if you were given a second chance to live?"

Mecca thought about lying to Lou when she answered the question. She wanted to tell him, "I will start my life off fresh, get a job, and leave the streets alone," but she figured he would know she was lying, so she might as well keep it real.

"I don't know. It's hard to say now with all that you've shown me. Where would I begin? I have no real friends except my aunt."

Mecca couldn't see Shamel's thoughts of him having sex with Ruby when Lou showed her Ruby's court date. He withheld showing Mecca that for a specific reason. He wanted to see how mentally prepared Mecca was before he showed her the ultimate betrayal. Mecca already saw the infidelity that Shamel engaged in with Karmen, but how would she handle betrayal from the only person she trusted?

"Revenge doesn't change what's already been done, Mecca. You have to realize that. You can't remove the past, you can only work on the future. No one loves you more than you can or do. I know you heard the saying, keep your friends close, but your enemies closer. Most of the time your friends are your enemies. Even your family," Lou said, staring into her eyes, seeing if she could read his thoughts.

"Why did you say 'even your family' like that? What are you trying to say, Lou?" Mecca yelled.

Lou began to second-guess revealing to Mecca what he was going to reveal. It could either make or break her, but he hoped that it would make her realize that nothing good comes out of evildoers. So he decided to reveal to her what he called the "Ultimate Betrayal."

Chapter Twenty-four

A continual dropping in a very rainy day
and a contentious woman are alike.
Proverbs 27:15

Langston Hughes Projects, 1982

"You like this dick, don't you!"

"Oh God, I love it! Don't stop! Please don't stop!"

"Whose pussy is this? Say whose pussy this is!"

"This is Darnell's pussy!" Ruby moaned as she was positioned in doggie style while Darnell rammed his large manhood in Ruby's vagina. After three hours of wild, sweaty sex, Ruby laid on Darnell's chest playing with his chest hairs.

"You got to promise me. Give me your word that you won't hurt anybody," Ruby said.

"C'mon, baby, you know my word is good. All I want is the stash of boy he got. I told you we're gonna get rich," Darnell replied, referring to the drugs he planned to get later that day.

Ruby turned over in the bed, and Darnell slapped her plump ass playfully as she reached on the floor and grabbed her blue Sergio Valente jeans and pulled out a set of keys. She rolled back over and handed the keys to Darnell. He kissed her on the lips and jumped out of the bed.

"Don't worry, ain't nobody gonna get hurt."

The next day, Darnell and his little brother wore masks and entered the Langston Hughes apartment using the keys Ruby gave him. He saw a little girl asleep on a bed in the corner of the living room. Well, he thought she was asleep, but the little girl saw the masked men enter the apartment. She closed her eyes and lay still, thinking they wouldn't see her.

The little girl thought her tactic worked when the two men walked past her and into her parents' bedroom, and she crawled under her bed. She heard the men talk loudly to her parents.

"Don't do anything stupid. Don't make us kill you. Get up slowly!"

Seconds later the little girl watched as her mother and father were led into the living room and made to sit next to each other on the couch.

One of the men tied them up with duct tape on their mouths, wrists, and ankles. The little girl then watched one of the men walk to the refrigerator and remove a plastic bag with a gray powder in it. Then she heard one of the men say, "You got the shit, Darnell?" The look on her father's face made the girl assume that her father knew the man called Darnell.

Her father tried to speak through the duct tape but couldn't. The guy Darnell appeared angry that the other man yelled his name out. Darnell yelled at him and her father was moaning loudly at Darnell. The little girl heard Darnell, when he removed his mask, tell her father that his days working for Stone were over.

Silently praying, the little girl made no noise while roaches crawled over her face and inside of her footie pajamas. She watched the tears flow down her mother's face and then she let out a low scream as the masked men pointed the gun at her father's head and pulled the trigger. She let out another low scream when the gun was pointed at her mother and the trigger was pulled.

The men left the apartment and drove in a custom van. Darnell pulled over and ran to a pay phone on the corner of Mother Gaston Boulevard and Sutter Avenue. A voice picked up on the first ring.

"Darnell, what the fuck did you do, mu'fucka!" the voice yelled.

"Ruby, they knew who I was. My stupid brother said my name!"

"My niece saw that shit! How could you do this to me?"

After receiving the call from the little girl named Mecca, Ruby rushed over to her sister's house to get her niece. She didn't want her niece talking to the cops. On the way over to pick up her niece, Ruby banged on the steering wheel of her Camaro. She cursed herself for letting Darnell talk her into setting her brother-in-law up.

Ruby just wanted to take Stone's dope from Blast so she and Darnell could start their own spot. Darnell fucked Ruby so good she couldn't resist telling him no. She wanted to do anything he asked so he could give her dick when she wanted it.

Ruby didn't consider herself a nympho; she just had a weakness for a man who made her have multiple orgasms. She blamed Ron for her weakness. He was her first lover and her first sexual experience, which was unforgettable. She didn't realize the power of an orgasm. It wasn't just the orgasm that did it. The feeling of a man's hard penis touching her G-spot drove her nuts.

Not too many men knew how to find her spot. The ones who did had Ruby at their mercy.

Ruby swore to herself that she would make Darnell pay for what he did. She didn't know who Darnell's little brother was but to this day, she wished she did know who he was. If she had killed him back then also, he would have never been able to kill Monique. The police got to him before Ruby could get her revenge. He was now serving twenty years to life for it.

Ruby also swore to herself that she would make sure Mecca had the best of everything. Mecca wouldn't want for anything ever. She was to never find out what Ruby did. So she made it her duty to hunt Darnell down and kill him so he could never tell anyone.

After that, the killing continued. Ruby killed her way to the top. She wanted to rid herself of all potential threats to what she was building for Mecca. She knew she wouldn't last long and eventually she would be killed or in jail, but before that could happen, she would make sure Mecca had all she needed.

"Nooo!" Mecca screamed at Lou. Lou held his head down and shook it back and forth.

Epilogue

For jealousy is the rage of a mans, therefore he will not spare in the day of vengeance.
Proverbs 6:34

Tah and Mo Blood crept around the villa that Ruby left to Mecca in the Hamptons. He knew the code to disarm the alarm system, and the two pit bulls Mecca had didn't bark when they recognized Tah's smell. He gave Mecca the pit bulls as a birthday gift when they were together.

Mecca was asleep naked while Shamel walked to the kitchen naked to eat some leftover baked macaroni and cheese and some cold chicken wings. He put the macaroni and cheese in the microwave and set the time for a minute and a half.

Shamel watched the macaroni heat up on a plate that spun around inside. There was a hissing sound a split second before his head exploded against the glass door. His body slumped to the floor after Mo Blood put the bullet in the back of his head from his black 9 mm Berretta with a silencer on it.

Tah crept into Mecca's room with Mo Blood behind him. When Mo Blood saw Mecca's naked body, he whispered, "Damn, she is thick, son!"

Tah tapped Mo Blood on his shoulder and put his finger to his mouth signaling for him to keep quiet. Tah pulled some rope out of a black Jansport book bag he had in his hand. He knew Mecca was a heavy sleeper, so tying rope to her headboard wouldn't wake her; it was tying her up that would be a problem.

Tah tied the rope to the oak wood headboard. He whispered to Mo Blood after he tied to rope to the board.

"Son, I'ma lay on top of her to hold her down; tie her hands to the headboard," Tah instructed. Lying on top of Mecca awakened her.

"Yo, what the fuck is you doing!" Mecca yelled, unable to see who was lying on top of her. Tah positioned his body horizontally across Mecca's stomach and chest. She recognized Mo Blood and figured it was Tah on top of her.

"Tah, get the fuck off of me!"

Mo already had one of her wrists tied to the headboard. She wouldn't let him get the other wrist. She was kicking and moving wildly. Tah had no choice, so he got off of her.

"Son, hold her feet!" With one hand tied, Mecca kicked and punched with her free hand.

"Tah, you bitch-ass nigga! Get the fuck outta my crib!"

Tah caught Mecca's free hand and held it. She couldn't fight against the strength of Tah. His time in prison lifting weights and taking supplements and eating protein bars had him strong and muscular. He put his arm around her throat and squeezed, putting her to sleep.

When Mecca's body went limp, he tied her feet with rope and tied the rope to the bedpost. He tied her other hand to the headboard. Mo Blood grinned and attempted to touch Mecca's private parts, but Tah swung his fist hard, landing a right hook on Mo Blood's jaw, knocking him unconscious.

After he tied Mecca to the bed, he slapped her on the face to wake her up. At first her vision was blurry, and then it became clear after a few seconds. Still a little disoriented, she stared at Tah dressed in a black Sean John velour suit with black on black Air Force Ones on his feet. He wore a white headband on his shiny bald head. Slowly her eyes drifted to the chrome .50-caliber Desert Eagle he pointed at her.

"Tah, why are you doing this? What did I do to you?" Mecca pleaded trying to loosen the ropes by tugging on them.

"Why you think, Mecca?"

"Just because we ain't work out together, that don't mean we couldn't be friends," Mecca lied.

She knew she couldn't be friends with Tah because she couldn't trust him. He violated her by messing with Tamika behind her back. They could never be friends. Mecca remembered what Ruby told her about letting people mess up one time and no more. She fell in love with Shamel. He was the man Tah could never be and Shamel treated Mecca the way Tah didn't know how.

Tah laughed hysterically. "That's what you think this is about? I couldn't care less if you were sucking my dick. This ain't about me being mad because you stop dealing with me."

"Then what do you want from me? Money? You robbing me, Tah?" Mecca asked.

Tah shook his head. "You got in way over your head, Mecca."

"Tah, what are you talking about?" Mecca cried. She looked into his eyes and she knew he was getting high off of ecstasy pills and Xanex mixed with codeine. She recognized the look from seeing him this way before.

"You're not your aunt, Mecca. She's gone."

"Put the gun away, Tah, and untie me, nigga. You high off them pills!"

Mecca yelled, trying to sound authoritative, thinking it would make Tah listen. She remembered Tah would leave her alone when she got angry just like Shamel did. Most of her life people feared when she got angry, the same way her aunt made people fear her.

Those days were over and Tah couldn't care less about that look Mecca had on her face. The look that Mecca got when she was about to hurt someone. Tah thought, *This bitch still think a nigga her flunky or something. She outta her rabbit-ass mind.*

"Bitch, I ain't your damn flunky!" Tah yelled his thoughts out loud.

"Tah, who the fuck said you was a flunky?" Mecca asked. "You my man, nigga, not no flunky. You listening to them lame-ass niggas you be with and they put shit in your head. Be your own man mu'fucka!"

Tah knew when Mecca said he was her man she meant it as a friend. She was saying it like another nigga would say, "that's my man," but Tah knew that was bullshit. She didn't give a fuck about him. He wrote her from jail plenty of times and never got a reply. She sent him money one time and no letters. He poured his heart out in some of the letters, knowing she was lying up with Shamel. He vowed to himself that she would pay for his broken heart. No one treated Tah Gunz like a scrub. No one.

"Fuck you, Mecca!" Tah pulled the trigger.

When the bullet hit Mecca on her forehead, everything went black.

Lou and Mecca stared at each other for a few minutes. Mecca saw two silhouettes walking toward Lou from behind him. When the two silhouettes reached Lou they separated, and one stood on one side of Lou and the other on the opposite side. Their faces lit up and Mecca saw a male and female in long white robes, and then she recognized the faces of her parents.

The image of Lou and her parents disappeared and Mecca's vision was blurred. She saw a shadow behind a bright light. Her eyes were blinking rapidly. When her vision cleared, Mecca was looking up at Shamel's grandmother.

"Nurse! Nurse she's up!" Grandma yelled. A short, middle-aged, Spanish nurse rushed into the hospital room and smiled at Mecca.

"Hay Dios mio, she's alive!" the nurse said excitedly.

Shamel's grandmother held her hands and head up in prayer. "Thank you, Jesus."

November 6, 2001

Ruby received her mail from the corrections officer sitting at a desk on the cellblock. She rushed to her cell, anxious to open the envelope from the courts. She knew it was the decision for the appeal. When she got to her cell she ripped open the envelope and her knees almost buckled as she read:

AND NOW, on this 6th day of November in the year 2001 it is decided that the petitioner Ruby Davidson's motion to vacate a sentence of Life imprisonment is granted. The warden of said prison where petitioner is currently confined is ordered to release prisoner C024688 upon receipt of this order.

Ruby's heart leapt out of her chest as she read the order vacating her sentence. She was free. She handed the paper to her cellmate.

"I did it, baby! I'm out!" Ruby yelled enthusiastically.

"That's great, baby!" Kima said excitedly, but was secretly happy to be getting rid of her bully of a cellmate.

"Did you hear anything about your niece?" Kima asked, changing the mood. With the smile and enthusiasm gone from Ruby's face, a grim expression took over. Ruby took the paper from Kima's hand.

"They said she's out of a coma, but she might be a vegetable for the rest of her life."

Shamel's grandmother smiled at Mecca and rubbed her hand. Mecca's head was wrapped in bandages, but being in a coma for a month all the swelling went down in her face. Tah shot Mecca three times: once in her chest, one in the side of her face, and once in the forehead. When she turned her face simultaneously with the first shot that hit her forehead, it just grazed the front of her brain.

"Baby, your aunt's appeal went through. She's coming home tomorrow," Shamel's grandmother said, thinking the news would bring a smile to Mecca's face.

Mecca heard the news but couldn't speak. She wanted to yell at Shamel's grandmother about everything she knew about her grandson, her aunt, and everybody who betrayed her. Instead, she stared at Shamel's grandmother's eyes blinking, and a tear rolled down her cheek.

Author Bio

Anna J., bestselling author of *My Woman, His Wife* and *Snow White*, has been a heavy hitter for six years in the book business. With gritty street tales such as *Get Money Chicks* and erotic short stories like "A Crime of Passion" (appearing in the spring 2010 anthology *The Bedroom Chronicles*) Anna is a versatile storyteller who has become a household name. A Philadelphian, born and raised, she proudly writes about her city. Anna, fondly referred to by her friends as Ms. J., is excited about the release of her sixth novel *Hell's Diva*, and is hard at work on her next book.

ORDER FORM
URBAN BOOKS, LLC
97 N18th Street
Wyandanch, NY 11798

Name (please print):_______________

Address:_______________

City/State:_______________

Zip:_______________

QTY	TITLES	PRICE
	16 On The Block	$14.95
	A Girl From Flint	$14.95
	A Pimp's Life	$14.95
	Baltimore Chronicles	$14.95
	Baltimore Chronicles 2	$14.95
	Betrayal	$14.95
	Black Diamond	$14.95

Shipping and handling: add $3.50 for 1st book, then $1.75 for each additional book.
Please send a check payable to:

Urban Books, LLC

Please allow 4-6 weeks for delivery

ORDER FORM
URBAN BOOKS, LLC
97 N18th Street
Wyandanch, NY 11798

Name (please print):_______________________

Address:_______________________________

City/State:_____________________________

Zip:__________________________________

QTY	TITLES	PRICE
	Black Diamond 2	$14.95
	Black Friday	$14.95
	Both Sides Of The Fence	$14.95
	Both Sides Of The Fencc 2	$14.95
	California Connection	$14.95
	California Connection 2	$14.95

Shipping and handling: add $3.50 for 1st book, then $1.75 for each additional book.

Please send a check payable to:

Urban Books, LLC

Please allow 4-6 weeks for delivery

ORDER FORM
URBAN BOOKS, LLC
97 N18th Street
Wyandanch, NY 11798

Name (please print):________________

Address:____________________________

City/State:__________________________

Zip:________________________________

QTY	TITLES	PRICE
	Cheesecake And Teardrops	$14.95
	Congratulations	$14.95
	Crazy In Love	$14.95
	Cyber Case	$14.95
	Denim Diaries	$14.95
	Diary Of A Mad First Lady	$14.95
	Diary Of A Stalker	$14.95

Shipping and handling: add $3.50 for 1st book, then $1.75 for each additional book.

Please send a check payable to:

Urban Books, LLC

Please allow 4-6 weeks for delivery

ORDER FORM
URBAN BOOKS, LLC
97 N18th Street
Wyandanch, NY 11798

Name (please print):_________________

Address:_____________________________

City/State:__________________________

Zip:_________________________________

QTY	TITLES	PRICE
	Diary Of A Street Diva	$14.95
	Diary Of A Young Girl	$14.95
	Dirty Money	$14.95
	Dirty To The Grave	$14.95
	Gunz And Roses	$14.95
	Happily Ever Now	$14.95
	Hell Has No Fury	$14.95

Shipping and handling: add $3.50 for 1st book, then $1.75 for each additional book.
Please send a check payable to:

Urban Books, LLC

Please allow 4-6 weeks for delivery

ORDER FORM
URBAN BOOKS, LLC
97 N18th Street
Wyandanch, NY 11798

Name (please print):_______________

Address:_______________

City/State:_______________

Zip:_______________

QTY	TITLES	PRICE
	Hush	$14.95
	If It Isn't love	$14.95
	Kiss Kiss Bang Bang	$14.95
	Last Breath	$14.95
	Little Black Girl Lost	$14.95
	Little Black Girl Lost 2	$14.95

Shipping and handling: add $3.50 for 1st book, then $1.75 for each additional book.

Please send a check payable to:

Urban Books, LLC

Please allow 4-6 weeks for delivery